A Pint of Murder

A Pint of Murder

ALISA CRAIG

PUBLISHED FOR THE CRIME CLUB BY

DOUBLEDAY & COMPANY, INC.

GARDEN CITY, NEW YORK

1980

Canada is a vast land of endless variety and frequent mystery. To a Canadian child growing up in another country, it was always the place where the stories came from. There were stories told by her mother, to whom the Saint John Valley was always Home pronounced with the capital letter; stories told by her father to whom the Maritimes had been the Happy Hunting Ground of his youth. Now that her parents' bodies are back in the place their spirits never left, she makes up her own stories. This is one of them. Pitcherville and all its inhabitants and doings are straight out of her imagination, therefore any resemblance to actual persons or places would be astonishing as well as unintended. At the time of writing there was no RCMP officer named Rhys working out of Fredericton, and no resemblance to any actual member of the RCMP is either implied or intended.

ISBN: 0-385-15838-6
Library of Congress Catalog Card Number 79-6659
Copyright © 1980 by Doubleday & Company, Inc.
All Rights Reserved
Printed in the United States of America
First Edition

To My Aunt
for her Ninety-first Birthday

A Pint of Murder

CHAPTER 1

"Aunt Aggie, are you all right?"

"Damn—fool—question."

The old woman on the floor retched again. The body jerked in convulsions, then was still. Agatha Treadway died as she'd lived, despising Marion Emery.

"She seemed okay at suppertime."

Marion wasn't being much help. She sat huddled on one of the dusty green plush chairs in the front hall, shivering in a baby-doll nightgown that was ridiculous on her lanky, middle-aged figure and in any case a bit optimistic even for July, although summers in eastern Canada are much milder than tourists are apt to expect.

"What did she eat?" snapped Dr. Druffitt. He was feeling, not for the first time, a powerful urge to land his wife's cousin a hefty blow across the starboard mandible.

"J-just the usual."

"The usual what? For God's sake, Marion, try to make sense for once in your life."

"Hell, Henry, how do I know? Something out of a jar from the cellar. String beans, I guess it was. And bread and butter and tea, same as always."

"Did you eat the same things?"

"I had a cup of tea and some bread and butter, that's all. I'd grabbed a bite at the Busy Bee when I got off the bus, knowing there'd be no hope of a decent meal from Auntie." Marion's shrug turned into a shudder. "Henry, she's not really dead, is she?"

"Here, cover yourself up." The doctor snatched a faded tapestry scarf from the hall table and slung it around the woman's thin shoulders.

"Of course she's dead. From the look of that kitchen floor, I'd guess food poisoning. She probably woke up with stomach cramps and came downstairs to mix herself a dose of baking soda, then it really hit her. Any of those string beans left, eh?"

"I don't know."

"Then go find out, can't you?"

"God, Henry, don't make me go back there again."

But Marion Emery was used to doing as she was told at the Mansion. She dragged herself off the chair and slumped down the drafty, dark hallway, looking every minute of her forty-six years, Dr. Druffitt herding her along like a snappish old collie. As they passed through the swinging door into the kitchen, they heard a rapping at the back door.

"Now who the hell is that?" Sidling close to the wall in order to avoid what was on the floor, Marion went over and snapped on the outside light. "Oh hi, Janet." She betrayed herself as a foreigner by pronouncing the name to rhyme with "gannet."

Janet Wadman herself, like a good New Brunswicker, used the gentler "Jennet." She looked as gentle as her name, though in fact she could be crisp enough if need arose. Her peach-blossom cheeks were the sort to show dimples if there'd been anything to smile about, and her baby-fine hair had turned to a soft, curly nimbus in the night air, showing bronze-brown glints under the naked overhead bulb.

Janet was the younger sister of Bert Wadman, who ran the farm next door, the Mansion's only neighbor out here on the hill. She was clutching a challis wrapper around her, a dainty rose-printed thing designed for a pretty woman, which Bert's wife, Annabelle, had given her a year and a half ago when Janet had gone away to an office job in Saint John. She'd loved the robe then. Now its roses were a trifle too exuberant for her pallor, the pattern too sweet to go with the more mature set of her mouth.

"I couldn't sleep," the purple smudges under Janet's dark gray eyes suggested she hadn't been sleeping for some time now, "and I heard the doctor's car drive in. Is she bad?"

Henry Druffitt had a mean streak in him. He stepped away so she could see into the kitchen. "What do you think?"

"Oh my God! What was it?"

"Henry says food poisoning," Marion answered for him.

"But that's crazy! She—I'll get a bucket of sawdust, eh?" Clenching her teeth, Janet ran for the woodshed. She had to get away from there long enough to pull herself together. When she came back a few minutes later, outwardly a bit more collected and carrying a galvanized pail in her hand, she found the others sniffing at a preserving jar they'd taken from the ancient high-domed electric refrigerator.

"They smell okay to me," Marion was saying.

"You can't go by that," Dr. Druffitt replied. "This would be botulism. It's far deadlier than ordinary food poisoning. Home-canned string beans are dangerous breeding grounds because of their exceptionally low acid content. Aggie ought to have known better."

"But Auntie canned them herself," Marion argued, "and you know how fussy she was."

"I also know she was eighty-seven years old. At her age she could slip up for once, couldn't she? Anyway, I'm going to send this jar down for analysis by the morning bus. I ought to take a sample of the stomach contents, too, I suppose. Get me a spatula and an empty container with a lid to it."

Janet had begun scattering sawdust over the mess on the floor, being careful not to get any on the old woman, whom she'd dearly loved.

"Couldn't you hold off till I got a specimen?" snapped the doctor.

"No, I couldn't." It was none of his business why. Janet wasn't going to tell anybody, ever, about that last time she'd gone out with Roy.

She'd been feeling queasy all that week, then she'd developed a stitch in her side. She'd thought she must have picked up a bug of some sort, and that it would go away if she kept working and made believe it wasn't there. But the pain had gotten worse.

By Friday she'd felt downright awful, but Roy had been planning a big smash to celebrate his birthday, and she couldn't bear to spoil it. For the past several months, Roy had been giving her every reason to believe his happiness depended on being with her. There'd been hints from certain of their coworkers that she wasn't the only girl who'd been led to think so, but naturally she put them down to jealousy.

So she'd had a bottle of champagne chilled and waiting when he came to pick her up, and had taken a few sips herself in the hope of quieting her stomach while he and her roommates drank the rest. Then they'd gone on to the restaurant, and the minute she got inside and smelled the food, she'd had to rush outside again and disgrace herself all over the sidewalk.

To make matters worse, a couple of chaps Roy knew had come along just then. She'd been too wretched to hear what they were saying, but she could guess what the laughter was about. And Roy had been furious. He'd shoved her into a cab, given the driver five dollars and her address, and stormed off.

Whether she'd managed to convince the man that she wasn't drunk but sick, she'd never know. In any event, he'd dropped her at a hospital emergency ward and driven away without offering to help her inside. She'd managed that somehow by herself and gone through the nightmare of getting admitted when she didn't know where she was and could hardly remember her own name for the pain. Roy hadn't even sent a get-well card.

It wasn't that he hadn't known about her ruptured appendix. As soon as she was able, Janet had sent word to the office. The boss's secretary had come right over on her lunch hour with a bunch of flowers, and been sweet about telephoning Annabelle and Bert. Alice and Moira had dropped by a few times after work and at last Janet had gotten up courage enough to mention Roy's name. Moira had given Alice a look and Alice had blushed and said, "Oh he's fine. I'll tell him you said hello," and that was the end of her great romance.

Only Janet wasn't the sort who could turn her feelings on and off like faucets and that was one of the reasons she couldn't endure the sight of that kitchen floor. She got out the mop and filled her pail with hot soapsuds, and fished out a tissue to wipe her tear-wet cheeks. "And furthermore," she sniffled angrily, "you can analyze till you're black in the face, but you'll never get me to believe Mrs. Treadway let those beans go bad."

"Who's the doctor here, you or Henry?" Marion retorted. "If Auntie didn't, then who did? That's one of her jars, isn't it? God knows I've seen enough of them."

"Yes, I know. She bought twelve dozen of each size the day she got back from her honeymoon, and never broke one in her life. She was so proud of those jars." Janet brushed away a last tear and went on swishing suds over the kitchen floor. Mrs. Treadway had been proud of her linoleum, too.

"Well, Aggie was long past her threescore and ten," said Henry Druffitt in that fretful voice which was one of his several unpleasant characteristics. "Her faculties weren't what they had been."

"She was sharp as a tack and then some," Janet insisted. "Marion can tell you that."

Certainly the niece had been here enough times to judge, though the aunt had done all she could to discourage Marion from inviting herself. "Sucking around after money," had been Mrs. Treadway's acid and wholly accurate estimate of this familial devotion, both in and out of Marion's hearing.

"Besides," Janet went on, "she knew perfectly well how careful you have to be about canning snap beans. Rank poison if you let the air get at 'em, she'd say. You've heard her, Marion."

Dr. Druffitt wasn't paying any attention. He wrapped his specimens in a clean cup towel and stuffed them into his black leather satchel. "Marion, I suppose you'll want to come back with me. Get your clothes on while I phone down to see if Elizabeth has the spare room ready, eh?"

"But you're not going off and leave Mrs. Treadway here on the floor?" cried Janet. "It's not decent!"

"Can't see where it's going to make any difference to her now," the doctor grumbled. "All right then, one of you help me carry her in on the dining-room table. I'll send Ben Potts up first thing in the morning. No sense dragging both of us out of a night's sleep."

He slid his hands under Mrs. Treadway's armpits and turned her on her back, letting the arms flap loose. Marion cowered away, but Janet bent and took the thin legs. This couldn't be doing her incision much good, but it was the last service she could perform for her old friend and that was what mattered.

Marion did summon up enough enterprise to go ahead and switch on the light over the dining-room table. As it shone down on the doctor's head, Janet couldn't help noticing how bald he'd gotten since she saw him last. Henry Druffitt was getting on in years. His wife must be middle-aged, too. It was hard for Janet to think of Mrs. Druffitt as being any age at all. She'd had the doctor's wife for a Sunday-school teacher, and always pictured her like the church steeple, rigidly upright and pointed in the proper direction.

Infallibility wasn't the husband's long suit, though. Henry had stepped into his father's practice after barely scraping through medical school, and hung onto it mainly because he'd had no competition until the new highway put the county hospital within practical driving distance. Now his patients preferred to take their more serious ailments to a place where diagnosis was more reliable and prognosis less dependent on a sound constitution and a hopeful disposition.

Annabelle Wadman was down at the hospital now, having surgery for what the older ladies of Pitcherville still referred to as "female complaints." She'd known for some time it would have to be done, and had timed the operation for the summer holidays, when her children could stay with their grandparents not far from the hospital, and be spoiled rotten.

Annabelle would be going to her folks, too, to recuperate and be close to her specialist for postoperative checkups. Originally they hadn't planned for Janet to come home and keep house for her brother. Molly Olson and some other neighbors from the village had promised to come up and lend a hand, and anyway Bert took off to be with his wife and the boys every chance he got. After her own illness, however, Janet had welcomed any excuse to get away from Saint John and Roy.

According to Annabelle, it was Dr. Druffitt's fault she needed the operation. He'd delivered her first baby and she'd never been quite right since. The doctor claimed it had simply been a difficult birth and nobody could have managed better. Janet, knowing her sister-in-law, was inclined to side with the doctor on that one though of course she'd never dare say so because she loved Annabelle in spite of everything. But she knew for a positive fact that Dr. Druffitt had to be wrong about Agatha Treadway's having killed herself with her own cooking.

The old woman's persnickety ways had been a family joke ever since Janet could remember, and long before. Those jars could no doubt be sold as antiques these days, but there wasn't a chip or a crack in any one of them. Mrs. Treadway had never used a sealer ring more than once, and she'd no more have fooled around with halfway methods than she'd have danced the black bottom on Sunday. She even used to boil the tongs employed to lift the scalded jars out of the preserving kettle. If those string beans had gone bad in the jar, then it wasn't Agatha Treadway who'd put them up, and that was that.

But if she hadn't canned them herself, then she'd never have eaten them. Forty-odd years ago, Mrs. Treadway's husband had opened a commercially processed tin of tomatoes with a patent can opener of his own invention, eaten its contents, and died. From that day on, the widow had bought nothing from any grocer except flour, sugar, salt, and tea. She'd gotten milk and eggs from the Wadman farm, churned her own butter, and made her own sourdough bread. She caught fish in the pond now and then, or ate home-cured bacon the Wadmans gave her, but mostly she lived on what she grew in her own garden.

When she got too old to tend her own plot, she'd been glad enough to accept fresh fruits and vegetables for canning from any neighbor who chose to share them with her, but nobody, not even Janet's late mother, had ever got her to taste a bite of cooked food after Charles Treadway died.

Yet Agatha Treadway had been fond of the Wadmans, fonder than she'd ever been of her own kin. She'd outlived both her brothers. For blood relatives, she had only the two nieces, Marion and Elizabeth, plus Elizabeth's daughter Gillian and grandson Bobby. Marion she'd openly scorned. Elizabeth Druffitt hadn't set foot inside the Victorian ark Pitcherville called the Mansion for fifteen years and more.

At least Marion's faithful treks up from Boston had kept her in the will. "She'll get her fair share," old Aggie had scoffed. "God knows she's worked hard enough for it." The half that was to have been Elizabeth's before the big fight would go to Gilly Bascom, the Druffitts' only offspring.

Not that there could be much left for anybody by now. Charles Treadway had run through most of a sizable lumber fortune financing his crazy inventions. The widow had been dipping into capital for years, to keep the Mansion from tumbling around her ears. Whatever she'd had, though, would stay in the family because Agatha had always believed in sticking by your own whether you could stand them or not.

It was going to be a lonesome old summer out here on the hill with Mrs. Treadway gone and Bert away so much and only Julius the cat for company. Janet gave the wet mop a final rinse and hung it back in the cellarway. She got a clean hand towel out of the drawer by the kitchen sink, wet and soaped one end of it, then went to the dining room and gently sponged the face and hands that were already like waxworks. She went upstairs for a clean sheet, a nice one with a crocheted edge, brought it back down, and spread it over the tall, still form on the dining-room table.

There was nobody here to help her. Marion had gone off in the doctor's car without a backward look, much less a tear for dear old Auntie. That didn't matter, Janet was crying enough for both of them. Her brother Bert would feel awful, too, when he found out. No sense in waking him tonight. One thing about bad news, as their own dead mother used to say, it could always wait till morning.

CHAPTER 2

"Janet, could you spare me a slice of bread?"

"Come on in, Marion," sighed Janet. "I'll warm up the teapot."

This was ten days after Agatha Treadway had been laid to rest, and Janet was beginning to wish she'd stayed in Saint John to nurse her sore belly and her broken heart. Watching Roy parade his new love couldn't be any more irksome than fetching and carrying for Marion Emery.

Bert, who didn't find neighborly hospitality onerous since he wasn't the one who had to cope with their new star boarder, was getting a good deal of amusement from Marion's staying on at the Mansion. "Hi, how's the heiress this morning? Found the hidden millions, eh?"

"Nope," mumbled their self-invited guest through a mouthful of Janet's homemade doughnut. "Still looking."

"Keep it up. It's good, healthy exercise. Don't know's it's good for much else." Bert went out to start the tractor, and she glowered after him.

"Great little kidder, isn't he? When I think of all the nights I've sat freezing to death on that lousy Boston bus, and for what? Five thousand bucks in Canadian money and a half share in a white elephant. I know damn well Auntie had a boodle stashed away someplace, and I'll find it if I have to take that moldy dump apart board by board."

"Marion, I've told you over and over you're wasting your time," said Janet, not that it would do any good. "You know better than I do how your Uncle Charles managed to get rid of what his father left him. Your aunt had her old-age pen-sion and that little bit left in the bank, and everybody around here was surprised she had that much. Gilly wasn't expecting any great windfall, was she?"

"How do I know what she expects? All she's doing is sitting down there on her backside expecting me to do the work for her. Boy, I wouldn't have wished a kid like her even on my cousin Elizabeth. Running off with that Bascom creep before she even got through high school, then crawling back with a brat on her hands after he ditched her. And holing up in that shack beside the diner instead of going home to that nice, big house when Elizabeth practically begged her on bended knee. But, no, Gilly had to be independent."

Marion bit savagely into another doughnut. "She's not going to let Elizabeth run her life, she says, but she sure doesn't mind letting ol' Mom foot the bills for the groceries. If it hadn't been for her folks, she and that kid of hers would have starved to death long ago."

Though she'd never been any great chum of Gilly Druffitt, Janet didn't like hearing Marion run the woman down like this. "Now, Marion, you can't say Gilly doesn't try. She works whenever she gets a chance."

"At what? Waitressing part-time at the Busy Bee when Ella's off on a drunk. Taking a course in poodle clipping when there isn't a poodle within fifty miles of this jerkhole. Now she's breeding dachshunds, for God's sake. Last year she was going to make a million bucks a week selling eggs. Then one of her hens got out of the pen and some kid ran over it in his jalopy and she bawled for a week and had to get rid of the rest because they weren't safe down there."

"I know. She brought them to us." Janet didn't add that she and her sister-in-law had had a quiet sniffle together over the tragic look on Gilly's thin little face as she dragged the makeshift crate of squawking poultry from her old Ford. The hens had proved to be incredibly poor layers, but Janet saw Annabelle was still protecting them from the stewpot.

Having drained the last dreg of tea and realizing that Janet had no intention of brewing any more, Marion set down her empty cup. "Well, I'd better get back to the mausoleum. Dot Fewter's coming up this morning, though why I asked her I don't know. Dot supposedly cleaned for Aunt Aggie every week, but I can't see any sign that she ever did anything. I'll probably get lung cancer from inhaling so much dust."

"Hold your nose," Janet suggested. "Dot's not too bad so long as you stand over her with a shotgun. Annabelle tried her for a while back in the winter, though she did say she'd have fared about as well tying a duster to the cat and chasing him through the house. Is that Sam Neddick bringing Dot now? His car just turned into your driveway."

"Yeah, I suppose so. Sam's supposed to fix a few leaks and cut the grass, but no doubt he'll be gone again before I can grab him. Janet, I don't know what I'm going to do over there. There's work that's absolutely got to be done, and the lawyers won't let go of a cent till we file a complete inventory. Elizabeth keeps yelling at me to get it finished, but she won't raise a hand herself. She's so damned proud of that grudge she's been holding for fifteen years that she still won't stick her nose inside the door of the Mansion. I was surprised she even showed up at the funeral, but I guess she wanted to make sure Aunt Aggie was safely planted so that her darling daughter could get her little hooks into her half of the Treadway millions. What a howl!"

"Won't Gilly come up and help you, eh?"

"She said she would, but then one of her dogs came down with the mumps or something so she has to sit and hold its crummy paw. I don't suppose you'd care to run over for an hour or so?" Marion interjected slyly.

Janet's first impulse was to snap the woman's head off. Then she reflected that it was a long way to dinnertime, that the house was clean and the washing done, that she hadn't an earthly thing to do here but sit and brood about Roy. She might as well go.

"All right. I'm not going to clean for you, but I'll help with the inventory. Should I bring a notebook and pencil, eh?"

"God, no! Uncle Charles left enough of his letterheads to

sink a battleship. Would you believe Treadway Enterprises Ltd? What a fruitcake! Okay, let's go before Dot falls asleep."

Janet followed Marion over to the Mansion, wishing it were Gilly instead of this endless complainer and all-around leech who'd moved up to the hill with her skinny little boy and her fat little dogs. At least they now had things in common. The six years' difference in age that had seemed so wide a barrier in school wouldn't matter now that they were both grown women who'd been ditched.

"Now, who the hell is that?" Marion broke in on Janet's bitter reverie, pointing to a rusty truck that had just pulled in behind Sam Neddick's rattletrap. A bizarrely attenuated and elongated man was climbing out, craning his neck to look up at the peeling gray paint on the house Pitcherville had once considered the acme of elegance.

Maybe this trip was going to be worthwhile, after all. "Oh haven't you ever met him?" said Janet with malicious glee. "That's Jason Bain."

"Bain? Isn't he the one Auntie was always talking about, who sues somebody for something about once a week? What's he want from me?"

"Anything he can get, most likely. He's not particular, long as it's free. Come on, let's find out."

They walked around to confront the man, who was now at the front door. Bain took his finger off the bell push and raised his noisome felt hat an inch or two.

"Miss Emery, I presume? Bain's my name. I don't b'lieve we've had the pleasure."

"The pleasure's all yours, mister," said Marion sourly. "What do you want?"

"I just stopped by to collect some property o' mine."

"Like what?"

"I'm lookin' for a patent right that was held jointly by me an' Charles Treadway. Accordin' to the terms of our agreement, it reverts to me on the widder's death."

Marion set her jaw. "Is that so? For your information, Mr.

Bain, nothing's going to leave this house till the inventory's been filed and we know exactly where we stand."

Bain shrugged. "I didn't come here lookin' to stir up trouble, but if I have to take legal action to protect my interests, I will. Might be kind of expensive for you to fight me an' lose, but that's your lookout, not mine."

Marion's hair had once been raven, and she'd made the mistake of trying to keep it that way. Against the dead black mass, her face showed white as a plaster cast. "I don't know what you're talking about. What's it for, anyway? I've never seen any patent. I wouldn't even know what one looked like."

"You'll know this one, 'cause my name's on it."

"Oh yeah? And what's that supposed to prove? You got anything to show you're entitled to the claim?"

"You bet your bottom dollar I have."

"Then fork it over."

"That ain't how I do business. You show me the patent, an' I'll show you the proof."

"Well, I haven't got it and I don't know where it is," Marion told him sulkily.

"That don't surprise me none. Stands to reason Miz Treadway wouldn't leave a valuable document layin' around loose. She had it hid away somewheres, an' if I was you, I'd start right this minute an' ransack this house from stem to stern. If that patent ain't in my hands by Thursday mornin', I'll be talkin' to my lawyer Thursday afternoon."

Bain didn't bother to tip his hat again. He swiveled his enormous length around, thumped down the worn wooden steps, folded himself inside his shabby pickup, and drove off. Marion stared after the smoke-belching truck.

"Can you beat that? If that old buzzard thinks he can scare me—" Clearly he could, and had. "Janet, what am I going to do?"

"Find that patent, I suppose."

"Then what? If he thinks I'm just going to hand it over to him like a dummy, he's got rocks in his head. How do I know he's entitled to any patent? The thing must be worth a bundle, or he wouldn't be putting up such a squawk."

Janet shook her head. "You don't know old Jase. He's perfectly capable of starting a lawsuit just for the fun of it. Anyway, you'd better find the thing. Where do you suppose it could be?"

"God knows. I've been through Uncle Charles's desk and every other place I can think of already. I don't remember noticing any patents, but maybe I skipped over them thinking they didn't count for anything. Looks as if I'll have to start all over again."

"But what about the inventory? Wouldn't the patent have to be shown to the lawyer along with everything else?"

Marion slumped into a chair. "I wish I'd never left Boston."

That went for both of them. "Come on, Marion," snapped Janet. "Sitting there feeling sorry for yourself isn't going to get the job done. Take a paper and pencil and start up attic. Look everything over and list as you go."

"It'll take forever."

"It sure will, if you don't get cracking. I'll begin down cellar. Where did your uncle keep all that stationery of his?"

Janet had made up her mind that Marion Emery was just about the most useless creature who ever encumbered the earth. Then she went through the kitchen and caught Dot Fewter taking advantage of the diversion caused by Bain's visit to get herself nicely settled with a box of store cookies and a mug of oversweetened tea.

"Come on, Dot, you're not getting paid to sit around stuffing your face. Help me take inventory."

"Huh?"

"We're going down cellar and list whatever we find there."

"I wouldn't know where to start."

"You don't have to know. I'll call things off, and you write them down. You can do that much, can't you?"

"I guess so." At least Dot was good-natured. She grinned as

she lumbered to her feet. "I'd just as soon go down cellar anyway. It's nice and cool there."

"I know." That was why Janet had elected to start at the bottom and let Marion stew in the stuffy, dusty attic. Besides, she'd always liked Mrs. Treadway's cellar, except for its peculiarly sticky floor.

One of Charles Treadway's many inventions had been a revolutionary kind of cement. As a test, he'd spread his first batch on his own cellar floor, and waited for it to dry. If he hadn't died forty-six years ago, he'd still have been waiting. The material had stood up well enough, to be sure, but anybody who stepped on it found his shoesoles spotted with a whitish deposit that was totally impossible to get off.

Virtually everything the old man had ever invented was a disaster. Even his one modest success, the improved can opener, had been the instrument of his own demise. Why, after all this time, was Jason Bain so impatient to get his claws on one of Charles Treadway's crazy patents?

Janet couldn't imagine. She also couldn't imagine why she'd thought it a good idea to make Dot Fewter join her in this inventorying. Dot, however, was all for it. Pleased at being assigned what she obviously considered a glamorous job for a change, she seated herself on an upturned nail keg and arranged her papers importantly on one end of the inventor's workbench.

"What shall I write?"

"Let's see." Janet gazed around at the clutter of seventy years and more, appalled at the task she'd so lightly undertaken. "You might as well put down one workbench for a start."

"One—workbench—for—a—"

"For Pete's sake, Dot, you needn't write every word I say. Just put down 'workbench.' Three rows of shelves. I suppose we've got to itemize all this stuff she put up, though I can't imagine anybody will ever dare to eat it now. Two pints tomatoes. She was almost out of them, poor soul. She loved tomatoes in the wintertime. Twelve pints peaches. Six pints pears."

"Wait a second. How do you spell 'twelve,' eh?"

"Make a No. 1 and put a 2 after it. And use a *p* for pints. She didn't use her quart jars any more. Too much for one old woman, she'd say. What's this stuff? Applesauce, I guess. Five pints." She'd get along faster listing them herself. "Two pints spinach or fiddleheads or something. These greenish old jars are hard to see into. Put down spinach, it's shorter. Fourteen jars—well, I'll be darned! Dot, what do you make of this?"

Dot climbed off her nail keg and pushed her nose close to the jar Janet was pointing at. After some deliberation, she pronounced her verdict. "It's snap beans."

"I can see that. But look at them. Here are thirteen other jars that have been snapped by hand more or less hit-and-miss, the way your mother or mine would have done them. But this jar's been cut very neatly and evenly with a knife, as the home-arts teacher taught us in school. Why should a woman who's been doing the same thing in the same way all her life suddenly turn around and do it differently?"

"I dunno," said Dot. "Say, can you beat that, eh? Wait'll I tell Ma! Mrs. Treadway always used to say a bean too old to snap was only fit for the pigs."

"I remember." Janet had a heart-wrenching picture of her old friend sitting out on the back doorstep, a heap of fresh green beans in the lap of her long white apron and her ropy hands going like clockwork, popping the crisp pieces into an old metal colander, tossing aside any bean that wouldn't break at a touch. "Nobody's ever going to convince me Mrs. Treadway did this."

"But if she didn't, who did?" argued the hired woman. "She'd never let anybody help her. I've offered a million times."

That was a lie, for sure. Janet doubted that Dot Fewter had ever volunteered for any task. It was true, however, that Mrs. Treadway would have refused. She wouldn't even have let

Annabelle, or Janet herself, touch her food once it had been picked and fetched over to the Mansion.

The color that she'd begun to get back in her cheeks suddenly drained out. "Here, Dot, you count all those empty jars and write down the number. I'm going upstairs for a minute."

She took the puzzling jar with her, cussing herself at every step for having blurted out her discovery. Now Dot would be right at her heels with an ear glued to the keyhole while she made the phone call she had to make. Mrs. Treadway had in fact died of eating botulinous string beans; the analysis and the autopsy had proved that. But had the beans that killed her been snapped or cut?

Janet knew better than to ask Marion. Either the niece wouldn't remember or else she wouldn't say. Dr. Druffitt had to be the one. Besides, he'd know where to send this second jar to be analyzed, as he had the first.

Mrs. Druffitt answered her call, impersonally agreeable as always. She didn't ask after Annabelle, which was understandable, but she did mention that she'd heard Janet had had emergency surgery down in Saint John, and was it her gall bladder? Doctor was out on a call just now, but he'd be in for his office hours and she hoped Janet wasn't in too much pain.

Janet said it was her appendix, knowing perfectly well that Mrs. Druffitt and at least one of the extraneous listeners on the party line were sure it had been something else. Since there was no hope of keeping her business a secret anyway once Dot found somebody to tell, she might as well not try.

"No, thanks, I'm making a good recovery. It's just that I'm over here at the Mansion helping Marion with the inventory and I've run across a—a little matter I'd like to ask Dr. Druffitt about."

"I see." Mrs. Druffitt was too great a lady to ask why Janet couldn't ask her instead, since it was she and not her husband who'd been Mrs. Treadway's blood relative. She did unbend so far as to say, "What does my cousin think about this little matter?"

"I haven't mentioned it to her yet," Janet confessed. "Marion's working in the attic and I've been down cellar. I thought I wouldn't bother her till I've got the doctor's opinion, since she has so many other things on her mind."

"That's very considerate of you, Janet. Marion does seem to be feeling the strain a great deal, eh? As we all are, of course. And so often things that appear important don't really amount to a hill of beans, do they? I'm afraid I'll be off to my club meeting, but if you could be here on the dot of two, I'm sure Doctor could spare you a moment."

"Thank you," said Janet. "I'll be there."

CHAPTER 3

When Janet told Bert at noontime that she'd like to use the car he'd said, "Sure, go ahead. Do you good to get off the place for a while."

Her brother no doubt thought she wanted to hobnob with her old pals in the village. In fact, as she started down the hill road, Janet was rather surprised to realize she didn't have a soul down there whom she particularly wanted to see. Growing up two miles out from the center, she'd been too far away to run with the pack even if her parents had let her, which they certainly wouldn't, having been middle-aged folk to whom a daughter fifteen years younger than the son before her had come as a considerable shock.

She'd got too much attention at home to mind the semi-isolation. Then Bert had brought Annabelle home, and she'd been fun, and then the babies had come and they'd been fun, too. Then, her senior year in high school, her father, who'd developed cataracts and really shouldn't have been driving at all, much less with his wife in the car, had got in the way of a logging truck. After that, Janet had decided maybe she'd like to go down to Fredericton to business college, and Bert and Annabelle had thought that was a sensible thing for her to do. And then she'd nursed Annabelle through a bad spell and then she'd taken the job in Saint John and by now the few friends she'd known had either married fellows from out of town or moved, like herself, to places where jobs were easier to find.

Certainly there wasn't much to do around Pitcherville. Some, like Bert, had their own farms and did pretty well.

Some of the men and a few of the women worked at the lumber mill five miles downstream. They fished, they hunted, they gardened, they did whatever odd jobs came along. One way and another, they got by.

Somebody must have picked up a few dollars doing roadwork since she was last home. They'd put down a lovely new pavement, which was nice but strange, as the road never got used much. Another governmental aberration, no doubt. What a pity they didn't have Charles Treadway still around to invent one of his super surfaces for them. He could have brought the whole country to a screeching halt in no time flat, thus saving the Conservatives, the Liberals, the N.D.P., and the rest a lot of fuss and bother. Whatever did Jason Bain want of that batty old inventor's patent?

The patent was the least of her worries. What really mattered was this jar of mismatched string beans. She parked in front of the one private residence on Queen Street that merited the description "imposing," and took her jar, discreetly masked in brown paper, off the front seat.

Mrs. Druffitt met her at the front door, dressed for her meeting in a lilac print dress, spotless white pumps with little bows on the toes, and an impressive Queen Mary toque of purple violets swathed in lavender veiling. Janet knew the outfit well. Mrs. Druffitt had been complaining for years that one had to keep wearing one's old clothes because one simply couldn't find anything fit to buy any more. It was generally agreed that Elizabeth Druffitt could find more excuses for not parting with a dollar than any other woman in Canada.

Preoccupied with pulling on her white nylon gloves and checking her handbag to make sure she had the notes for her little speech of introduction to the distinguished speaker of the day, the doctor's wife had no time to spare for Janet.

"Good afternoon, Janet. Please go right on in. I thought I heard Doctor putting the car away in the carriage house just now, but I'm so rushed I didn't take time to look. They've stuck me with the job of pouring out, unfortunately."

As if she didn't know every other member of the Tuesday

Club would cheerfully give a back tooth to preside over the teapot. Annabelle had never been invited to join that august group, of course, and Janet never expected to be. Gripping her jar, she nodded farewell to the lilac print as it swished down the well-swept brick walk, and went into the waiting room.

The house Elizabeth Druffitt had inherited from her parents was as gloomily grand as the Mansion must have been in its heyday, and a great deal better kept. Its furnishings hadn't changed in this century, except that pictures of Edward VII and Queen Alexandra, George V and Queen Mary, George VI and Queen Elizabeth, and Queen Elizabeth II and Prince Philip had been added in proper succession to the steel engraving of Queen Victoria and Prince Albert. King Edward VIII was conspicuously absent.

This place looked like a museum and felt like a funeral parlor, Janet thought as she settled herself and her perturbing burden on a slippery black horsehair sofa with crocheted antimacassars pinned to the back. No wonder Gilly had balked at bringing her son back here to live. What must it have been like for that only daughter, growing up inside this well-dusted tomb?

The hands on the red marble mantel clock pointed to exactly two when she sat down. She watched them swing around to five past, ten past, then a quarter past the hour. It certainly was taking Dr. Druffitt a long time to put that car away. Perhaps he'd stopped in the kitchen for a snack or something, but why didn't he at least poke his head in to see whether any patients were waiting? Janet began to get annoyed. She coughed once or twice, and when nothing happened she got up and tapped diffidently at the office door.

Still nothing happened. She knocked louder. At last she turned the knob and said, "Dr. Druffitt, are you—"

Then she saw the body on the floor. The crumpled mat at its feet told a clear story. The parquet floor was waxed slick as a curling rink. Dr. Druffitt must have skidded on that braided mat and bashed his head against the corner of the desk.

Janet knelt beside him, wondering if she ought to loosen his collar or something before she called for help. But something about the look of the man told her he was beyond any help she could get. Steeling herself, she slipped a hand inside his vest to feel for a heartbeat but could find none. She remembered something she'd read once, took the mirror out of her purse, and held it to his mouth. There was no clouding of breath. She hadn't really expected any.

But why hadn't she heard the crash when he fell? She'd been sitting right outside the whole time. Unless it happened during those few moments when she and Mrs. Druffitt had stood talking out at the front door. How dreadful, the husband lying dead and the wife tripping off to pour tea in her violet toque!

"Oh my God," Janet thought. "I'll have to go over there and tell her."

Janet knew where the Tuesday Club met, in the vestry of the Reformed Baptist Church. How could she face that group of respectable ladies with a horror tale like this? How could she leave the doctor lying here alone while she went? What if some child were to come in and find him like this, or an elderly person with a bad heart?

At last her head began to function again. Janet knew what she must do. She'd telephone to Fred Olson.

Olson was Pitcherville's town marshal, as well as its auto mechanic and sometime blacksmith. His police duties had never amounted to more than locking up the usual Saturday-night allotment of drunk-and-disorderlies or ticketing the odd Yank for admiring the scenery at sixty miles an hour, but he was a decent soul and better than nobody.

By the time she got him on the line, her voice was shaking so that he had a hard time understanding the first word or two. "Fred, this is Janet Wadman. I'm down here at Dr. Druffitt's office and you'd better come right on over. He's—I was waiting and he didn't come out so I knocked and then I opened the door and—for God's sake, will you hurry?"

She couldn't stay there. She went back to the waiting

room. It was terrible, being there alone with all those kings and queens staring down at her. Why didn't anybody else come? Surely Dr. Druffitt must have had a few patients left.

▼ It was too nice a day to get sick, that was why. It was too nice a day to be finding things in people's cellars one didn't want to find. Now she'd never know if that jar Dr. Druffitt had sent to be analyzed was a mate to the one she had here in a bag from the Dominion Stores. She'd never know for sure that this was how Agatha Treadway was murdered.

She might as well admit what she was thinking. Somebody had prepared those string beans wrong on purpose, and put them where Mrs. Treadway would find them, and eat them, and die. Two jars had been left in the cellar because there was a chance Mrs. Treadway might use the first before it had time to go bad. But there had been time enough.

Then why didn't the murderer come and take the second jar away? Maybe he, or she, had been too scared. Nobody had expected Marion Emery to stay on at the Mansion after her aunt died to hunt for that assuredly mythical hoard. Maybe the person hadn't realized the vegetables were prepared in a different way from the rest. It wasn't the sort of thing most people would notice.

Mrs. Treadway herself wouldn't have noticed. Her eyes had failed badly, though she'd tried to hide the fact for fear her nieces would clap her into an old-folks' home and help themselves to what was left of her property. But the Wadmans, who knew her so well, realized that during the past several years she'd been managing more by what she knew than by what she saw. Around the Mansion she could lay her hands on anything she wanted. She could still fix her own food and she'd eat whatever came from one of her own jars because she'd be sure it was safe. Only that last time, she'd been wrong.

Cutting beans in bunches was the quick, modern way. Only a really fussy cook like Annabelle or an old-fashioned one with time on her hands would bother to snap them one by one, feeling for perfect freshness. A would-be murderer who did home canning by modern methods would most likely chop them without thinking. One who did none at all might do the same because that was how canned or frozen beans came and he'd think that was the only way. Or somebody who knew perfectly well that Mrs. Treadway always snapped her beans might deliberately have cut the prospectively lethal string beans as a warning signal to himself.

After all, there'd been no telling when Mrs. Treadway might open that particular jar. She'd never been inhospitable. Anybody who happened to be around at mealtime would have been invited to share her meager fare. It would be hard to refuse the vegetables because there wouldn't be much else to eat. Yet to taste that particular serving would be a dangerous thing to do.

Who was apt to eat at the Mansion? Janet herself had, on any number of occasions. Annabelle used to go over often enough when the kids were at school and Bert off somewhere and she thought the old lady might like company. Gilly Bascom came once in a great while. Marion was there a lot, of course, and had to eat what was set in front of her or go hungry. Sam Neddick must have taken some of his meals with Mrs. Treadway since he did her chores and made his home in her hayloft, although since he was also Bert's part-time hired man, he usually preferred the more bountiful fare at the Wadmans'.

Dot Fewter couldn't be left out, either. Dot always lugged a horrible lunch of baloney sandwiches on store-bought bread when she came to clean, if such her feeble efforts could be called, but no doubt she'd have accepted whatever else was offered on top of that.

On the face of it, Marion and Gilly were the likeliest suspects. Both knew they stood to inherit. Both were always hard up for cash. Both had every chance to get at Mrs. Treadway's food supply.

But so did anybody else. The cellar was never locked. Anyone with a little luck and a lot of nerve could sneak in there some dark night, pinch a couple of empty jars, fill them up, and put them on the shelf with the string beans that were already there. It could be done in one trip by bringing the prepared beans in some other container and filling the jars on the spot. One wouldn't have to be fussy about how it was done, since the whole object was to let the food spoil. A child with a bike could manage—Bobby Bascom, for instance.

Gilly's misbegotten son was almost eleven by this time. Janet had heard that Bobby'd already been in trouble a few times for throwing rocks at Pitcherville's few street lights, swiping fruit from orchards, letting air out of people's tires; nothing serious but nothing that augured well for his future behavior. Annabelle thought it was plain awful the way that boy was being dragged up by the bootheels. Gilly didn't seem to have any control over him, and the grandparents showed less interest than a person might expect them to.

That was Bobby's grandfather lying dead in there. Janet wished she knew where the boy was now, and where he'd been twenty minutes ago. Could he have been poking around the office, by any chance? Might he have thought it funny to hide under the desk or somewhere, then reach out and give that treacherous little mat a yank?

Why should he think it was funny to do a thing like that? He was old enough to realize the possible consequences. Maybe he didn't do it to be funny. Kids could harbor grudges as well as grownups, and Janet had had a little sample last night herself of how nasty the doctor could be.

Bobby might even have thought he was doing something great for his mother. He might know something about a jar of string beans and a much-needed inheritance. He might very well have heard through the village grapevine that Janet Wadman was coming to show his grandfather something strange she'd found in the cellar up at the Mansion. Little pitchers had big ears.

Janet found she was having a hard time trying to swallow the coincidence that Dr. Druffitt had died just when he did. It was, however, frighteningly easy to credit the possibility that somebody hadn't wanted him to see that jar. If Bobby

Bascom could have heard about her errand, so could lots of other people. If he could have done that stunt with the mat, so could others.

A doctor's waiting room was a public place. Anybody could walk in through the waiting room. Everybody knew this was Mrs. Druffitt's club day, and that she'd be upstairs getting herself dolled up for the occasion. Everybody knew Dot Fewter wasn't working here today. Everybody knew everything about everybody, in Pitcherville. Somebody might still be lurking close by, wishing Janet would leave so that he could make his getaway. Why hadn't she thought of that sooner? She was almost out the front door when Fred Olson barged in and stopped her.

"What happened, Janet?"

"We're supposed to think he slipped on the mat and banged his head."

Fred either didn't catch the implication or chose to ignore it. He opened the office door and stood gazing down at the thin, elderly body sprawled on the gleaming parquet. "Poor old Hank. Never knew what struck him, I don't s'pose. That's a blessin', anyhow."

He knelt and prodded at the back of the skull, his blackened stubs of fingers tender as a mother's. "Yep, dent there you could get your fist into. Looks as if there's nothin' to do now but send for Ben Potts."

"Ben Potts?" cried Janet. "You can't just bundle him over to the undertaker without a doctor's certificate, can you?"

"No, I guess not, come to think of it." Olson scratched his raspy chin. "I might get hold of ol' Doc Brown. You prob'ly ain't heard he's back in town. Livin' with his married daughter Amy out beyond the Jenkins place."

"Dr. Brown? I didn't even know he was still alive. He must be crawling on for ninety."

"So what? He's still a doctor, ain't he? Might perk the ol' geezer up to make one last house call. You told Elizabeth yet?"

"No. I—it didn't seem right to leave him alone. I thought

I'd better call you first." Janet realized she was backing away from the body. She supposed she couldn't blame Olson for backing away from such a ghastly responsibility.

"Better get 'im up on the examinin' table an' haul a sheet over 'im before she comes. Be an awful shock to her, seein' him like this. Ben won't be back till suppertime. He's got a funeral over to West Jenkins." He bent and picked up the smaller, slighter body and swung it around toward the black leather-covered table.

"Watch out for his head!" Without quite realizing why, Janet put out her hand to shield the skull from the edge of the desk.

"Can't hurt it no more'n it is already," the marshal said grimly, but Janet wasn't paying any attention. Almost of their own accord, her fingers were exploring the shattered cranium.

"Fred, feel this dent again."

Reluctantly, he did. "It's busted all to hell an' gone, sure enough. What more do you want me to say?"

"Feel the shape of the break, I mean. Don't you notice how round and smooth it is? Shouldn't it be more—more angular? Like a hard edge would make?"

"How should I know? I'm no doctor."

"Neither am I, but I've fried enough eggs in my day to know that if I whack them with the round bowl of a spoon it makes a different sort of break than if I crack the shell on the edge of the frying pan, and so do you. Can you honestly believe the sharp corner of that desk wouldn't at least cut into the flesh and leave some kind of ridge or something?"

Olson prodded again, a worried expression on his red pudding of a face. "Criminy, Janet, I dunno what to think. What else could it have been? There's nothin' else in the way he could o' fell on. Maybe his hair—"

"What hair?"

The marshal's jaw dropped. He stared down at his old friend as if he'd never seen him before. "Lord A'mighty, I never realized. I can remember when Hank had corkscrew curls down to his waist. Had 'em myself, not that I wanted 'em. Forty years before you was born, I s'pose."

He sighed, picked up a clean sheet that had been lying ready beside the examining table for the patient who was never going to come now, and tucked it over his lifelong pal. "You go on over an' break the news to Elizabeth, Janet. I'll stay here an' try to get hold of Doc Brown."

Anxious as she was to get out of that place, Janet hesitated. "Fred, there's something else I have to tell you." She got her paper bag from the horsehair sofa, and showed him the jar. "Dot Fewter and I found this in Mrs. Treadway's cellar this morning."

He shrugged. "Seems as likely a place as anywhere else."

"Fred, listen to me. You know what Mrs. Treadway died of."

"Yep. Poisoned string beans."

"And you know how fussy she always was about what she ate."

"Yep. Fat lot o' good it did 'er in the end, eh?"

"All right, now take a look at this jar. Notice it's full of string beans. Notice that they've all been cut into nice, even pieces with a knife, like the ones you'd get in a frozen-food package."

"So?"

"Is that how your mother would have fixed hers?"

Olson shoved back the ratty tweed cap he was wearing and scratched his head. "'Pears to me she snapped 'em in 'er fingers."

"I expect she did. My mother did, too, and I've watched Mrs. Treadway do it ever since I was a little kid. Furthermore, there were thirteen other jars on the shelf beside this one, and every single bean in them had been snapped. Do you see what I'm getting at?"

The marshal scratched his head again. "Maybe she got tired o' doin' 'em all the same way."

"And maybe pigs have kittens. Look, Fred, I knew Mrs. Treadway as well as anybody in this world did, and there never was a woman more set in her ways. She had certain ways of doing things, and she wasn't about to change for anybody. I remember saying to her once, 'Mrs. Treadway, let me show you a new trick I learned in home arts,' and she said to me, 'No, thank you. I learned enough new tricks while my husband was alive. I'll stick to what I know is going to work.' "

Olson emitted a snort of laughter, then glanced into the office and looked embarrassed.

"Furthermore," Janet went on, "I was there and saw the jar she'd eaten from, after Marion Emery and Dr. Druffitt took it out of her fridge. It was one of her own preserving jars and a mate to this one. I couldn't be mistaken about that, because she'd had them for sixty years or more, and they haven't been on the market in ages. There probably aren't any others like them in the whole province."

"Did you see any of the beans that were left in it?"

"No, I didn't. Dr. Druffitt wrapped it in a cup towel and put it into his bag. That's why I came down to talk to him today. I meant to show him the one I'd found and ask if the beans were cut like these, because if they were, it's dollars to doughnuts somebody put them there on purpose to kill her."

The marshal took the jar out of her hand and stared into its murky depths. At last he shook his head. "I dunno, Janet. Sounds crazy to me."

"Of course it's crazy, Fred. Whoever claimed murder was sane? All the same it *was* murder, just as if somebody'd held a loaded gun to her head and pulled the trigger. And furthermore, you've got another one on your hands right in that office, and you know it as well as I do. And I'm very much afraid it's because of me and this jar that Dr. Druffitt was killed."

"How do you figure that?"

"Because Dot Fewter was with me when I found the jar and fool-like, I showed it to her instead of keeping my mouth shut. Then I called up Mrs. Druffitt to see if the doctor was going to be in, and she asked me point-blank if I was in pain because of course she knew I'd had that operation for my appendix down in Saint John, so I had to say no, I was all right but I wanted to ask the doctor about something I'd found in the cellar. Lord knows how many people were on the party line, and you can be darn sure Dot Fewter was burning up the wires to her mother the minute my back was turned. You know what that pair are like. Annabelle calls them the Maritime Network."

"Well Janet—"

"And you can't deny it's a bit too much of a coincidence, his turning up dead when I walk in here with this jar in my hand. You know as well as I do that he couldn't possibly have got that sort of injury by hitting the desk. It's my guess that somebody came at him from behind with something round and heavy, like the handle of that big brass poker right over there by the fireplace. They knocked him down, then dragged the body over by the desk and rumpled the rug under his feet to make it look as if he'd slipped."

"Aw Janet," an uneasy grin crept over Olson's face. "You been travelin' with the wrong kind o' crowd down there in Saint John, eh?"

If he'd wanted to get under her skin, he couldn't have picked a more successful way. Janet slammed the jar back into the bag and marched for the door. "Have it your own way, Fred. I've said my piece."

"Now, wait a minute. Don't go flyin' off the handle. Gimme time to think, can't you? S'posin' I did pick up that there telephone right this minute an' call the Mounties. What am I s'posed to tell 'em? At least we might as well wait an' hear what the doctor has to say."

Janet sniffed. "That old dodo? If he's still able to talk, he'll tell you whatever he thinks you want to hear. The only thing he ever knew how to treat was hypochondria. Couldn't you find a doctor who's halfway competent? Isn't there a provincial coroner or somebody?"

"Janet, how about if you simmer down an' use your head for somethin' besides a hatrack? You know damn well what's goin' to happen if I go stirrin' up a stink an' it turns out to be nothin' but your imagination. Maybe you don't give a hoot because you got a job back in Saint John, but what about me an' Bert?"

"Oh Fred, I hadn't thought of it that way." Living away from a small town, she'd forgotten what a deadly weapon gossip could be.

"Well, you better think of it," said the marshal. "Don't think I'm backin' down on this thing because I'm not. That jar of beans is evidence. That dent in Hank's skull is evidence. But they don't add up to a tinker's damn till we get a little more to go on. Look, Janet, me an' Hank Druffitt was babies together. If somebody killed him like you said, I want the bugger caught a damn sight worse than you do. But I can't go ahead an' start draggin' in outsiders till I'm pretty damn sure I got a reason to. I got a wife an' kids to think of, an' so does your brother."

Fred was talking sense, she had to admit. If he were to get the Mounties up here on Janet Wadman's say-so, all Pitcherville would be in an uproar. If they found nothing, Elizabeth Druffitt would work up her pals at the Tuesday Club to hound the marshal out of office for spreading scandal about her family. Olson would never get another car to fix. He'd have to move away somewhere and start over. Fred was too old a man for that. And Bert Wadman wouldn't be any too popular, either.

"I'll tell you what," the marshal went on, "you leave that jar with me. I'll go through Hank's files an' see if I can't put my hand on that report about Mrs. Treadway, eh? Then I'll send this jar to the same place. If they tell me it's spoiled like the first one, an' if the doctor thinks there's somethin' funny about that hole in Hank's head like you say, I'll have some justification for gettin' 'em in here."

The Royal Canadian Mounted Police would come if Fred asked them, no doubt about that. Any local law-enforcement official had a right to call on them for help with a problem that was beyond his resources to solve. But to have the Mounties in would be to acknowledge publicly that something was very wrong indeed, and the righteous folk of Pitcherville would envision the finger of scorn and derision being pointed at their village from Saint Stephen to Dalhousie. They wouldn't like that one bit, and they'd like it a great deal less if the whole case fizzled out and left nothing but a mighty stink behind. Much as Janet hated to admit it, Fred Olson was showing more common sense than she had, up to now.

CHAPTER 4

Breaking the news to the doctor's widow was less of an ordeal than Janet had anticipated. Mrs. Druffitt only said, "Oh Janet!" in a shocked whisper, then sank back in a chair and shut her eyes. At once the other ladies clustered around and Janet edged toward the door. Except for Mrs. Potts, who naturally took a professional interest in the details of the demise, nobody even noticed her leaving.

It was a relief to get into the car. She only wished she could get away from her thoughts so easily. She'd been a fool not to consider the consequences before she came charging down here with that jar of string beans. If it hadn't been for her interference, Henry Druffitt might still be alive.

And if it hadn't been for somebody else's interference, Agatha Treadway might also be alive. What was a person supposed to do?

One thing she probably ought to have done was track down Gilly Bascom and tell her about her father before she got the news third- or fourthhand from old Ma Fewter or somebody. Janet would have gone back and done it if not for that sneaking suspicion about Gilly's maybe knowing already.

It would have been so easy. There were two doors to the doctor's office: one from the waiting room and the other from the back hallway. The windows weren't far from the ground, and Mrs. Druffitt had let the hedges grow up high to keep the riffraff from peeking in. Moving the body around that polished floor couldn't have been any great job. That had been a clever blow, though, or else a lucky one, not to draw any blood and leave stains in the wrong place.

By the time Janet got home she was shivering. She made herself a cup of tea, but it didn't seem to help. When Bert came in from the barn, he immediately said, "What's the matter, Jen? You look like the skin of a nightmare dragged over a gatepost."

"I had sort of a bad experience this afternoon." She might as well tell him before somebody else did. "I went down to see Dr. Druffitt and found him dead in his office."

"For God's sake! What happened?"

"It appeared he'd slipped on one of those dinky little mats Mrs. Druffitt keeps strewn around, and cracked his skull on the edge of the desk."

She wasn't lying. That was how it had appeared.

"Can you beat that? Cripes, that's enough to take a rise out of anybody."

Bert shook his head. He had brown hair like hers, only less fine in texture and less apt to crimp up in the damp. The family resemblance was obvious although Bert was so much the elder, a full head taller, and at least fifty pounds heavier. They made an attractive pair. Annabelle always claimed she'd married Bert for his looks instead of his money, and Bert always said it was a darn good thing she had, though in fact the farm was doing pretty well thanks to his hard work and expert management. It would be a crime to cause him any more grief than he'd had already.

He reached into the cupboard for the rum bottle. Bert was no great drinker, but this one tot before supper was a ritual. As he went to get a tumbler, he stopped short.

"Say, what were you doing down to Druffitt's, anyway? That operation isn't giving you any trouble, is it?"

"Oh no." She had her lie all thought up. "It's just that I'm supposed to have somebody take a look at the scar and make sure it's all right. I know darn well it's healing fine, so I thought he'd do as well as anybody. You'd better go wash up if you intend to. Supper's almost ready."

"Okay. Give me five minutes. Oh hi, Sam. Come on in."

The hired man had manifested himself in the kitchen doorway without sign or sound, as was his wont. Automatically Bert poured another tot, and Janet began to set another place. Sam took the rum but shook his head at the food.

"Don't bother for me, I ain't got time. Ben Potts needs me to lend a hand down at the funeral parlor. She wants Hank laid out there."

Bert looked surprised. "Not in his own parlor? It's not like Elizabeth Druffitt to go against custom."

Neddick looked around, as if for a place to spit, couldn't find one, and politely refrained. "Guess the bitch don't want nobody wearin' out 'er carpets."

Even though Sam Neddick punctiliously did chores for the Druffitt household every week, there was open enmity between him and the mistress. Sam claimed Elizabeth owed him back wages for some extra work he'd done; she vowed she wouldn't pay because he'd never finished it to suit her. The incident had occurred before Janet left for business college, but the grudge was good as new on both sides.

"Understand it was you that found 'im, Janet."

"Yes, I did." She turned to the stove and became very busy prodding the potatoes.

"Let her alone, Sam. She's none too happy about it, as who would be?" said Bert.

Neddick set down his empty glass. He knew Bert wouldn't offer him another, and clearly Janet wasn't going to gratify his curiosity. "Well, I better be goin'. You want me tomorrow, Bert?"

"If you can spare the time. We've got to fix those rotten fenceposts in the upper pasture before we can put the cows to graze there."

Sam Neddick's shrug might have meant anything or nothing. "By the way, Bert, Fred Olson wants all the Owls down to the meetin' room tonight. Hank bein' a Past Grand Supreme Regent, we got to march in solemn procession behind the casket. Fred says we better practice so's we don't go makin' damn jackasses of ourselves in church."

"Oh gosh, Bert," said Janet, "I took your Owl tunic over to

the dry cleaner's last week. Annabelle told me to. She said you'd spilled something down the front at the Dominion Day parade. Beer, most likely. I'll have to drive over tomorrow and pick it up."

Her brother was none too pleased. "Why couldn't you wash it yourself?"

"And have those darn fool chicken feathers molting all over the gizzard of Annabelle's new washing machine?"

"You could have done it in the sink."

"And clogged the drain."

Sam knew the Wadmans never had really exciting arguments; they were too good-natured a family. He eased himself out without waiting to hear who won. Bert went to wash and change for the meeting. Janet began banging the pots and pans around, furious at Fred Olson. Here he was with a murderer running loose, and all the fool could think of was putting on a show at the current victim's funeral.

Bert, scrubbed and handsome in a clean flannel shirt and fresh chino pants, was taking his place at the table when somebody knocked timidly at the back door. Janet made a face.

"There's our star boarder again. I might have known." She raised her voice. "Come in, Marion. We're just sitting down."

A smaller voice replied, "It isn't Marion."

Janet went over and opened the door. "Why, Gilly Bascom! I thought you'd be at your mother's."

"I've been." The unexpected visitor slumped into the wooden chair Bert pulled out for her. "I've been listening to my dear mother moan about being a poor, lone widow till I couldn't endure another minute of it. If she'd said, 'You know it was your dear, dead father's wish' one more time, I'd have hauled off and belted her one across the mouth. Mama doesn't give two hoots, really. She'd never even notice Papa's gone if he hadn't given her another excuse to get at me about moving back with her."

Gilly's birdclaw hand clutched at a fold of the clean tablecloth. "I wouldn't go back there if she dragged me feet first.

Before I'd let my kid grow up under the same roof with her, I'd kill myself and him, too!"

Bert picked up the rum bottle again and splashed some into the fresh tumbler Janet quickly held out to him. "Here, take a swig of this. Good for what ails you."

He had to help her get the glass up to her mouth. She shuddered and coughed as she gulped down the spirit. "Ugh! Thanks, Bert. I'm okay."

She certainly didn't look it. Janet eyed her old schoolmate worriedly, wondering not for the first time how the imposing Mrs. Druffitt had ever hatched out a lone chick as forlorn as this one.

Gilly was about half her mother's size, with her father's washed-out coloring and small features framed in a frizz of bleached hair that showed an inch or so of mouse color at the roots. A ring of eaten-off lipstick outlined a soft, weak mouth. The huge gray eyes that should have been her real beauty were so plastered with makeup they looked like two burnt holes in a blanket. She had on a black pullover of sleazy nylon jersey and runover high-heeled shoes, white with dust from the road. She might have been a ten-year-old dressed up in her mother's old clothes, instead of the mother of a ten-year-old son.

She might also be a murderess. Nevertheless, the sight of her made Janet's heart ache. "Here, Gilly, I'll fix you a plate. What you need is a hot meal under your belt."

"Thanks, Janet, but I couldn't, honest. I've got to get back before Mama sends a posse after me. What I came for was to ask you and Bert a favor."

"Of course, Gilly. Anything we can do."

"I was wondering if you'd let me bring Bobby up here till after the funeral. I'd like to keep him out of the hullabaloo as much as I can. Maybe," she sniffled a bit, "he can feed the hens or something."

"Sure thing," said Bert a shade too heartily. "Glad to have him. We'll bed him down in the boys' room and he can play with their trains and stuff. He'll like that, I bet. You come, too, if you want."

"Don't I ever! But I wouldn't dare leave my own place. Schnitzi's expecting her pups any time now and I've got to be right there when it happens in case anything goes wrong. If I lose that litter, I'm done. Every nickel I could scrape together is tied up in those pups."

She tried to laugh. "Papa used to slip me a few bucks now and then when he happened to hold a winning hand for a change, but of course I couldn't expect a poor, lone widow to support two establishments on her few remaining pennies."

Gilly hauled herself out of the chair. "Well, I'd better get cracking. Mama wants me to go over to the funeral parlor in a while and help her heckle Ben Potts."

"I'm going down to the Owls later," Bert offered. "I'd be glad to stop by your place after the rehearsal and bring Bobby back here, eh?"

"That's sweet of you, Bert, but I'd sort of like to keep him with me tonight. I thought I'd feed him and get him straight to bed before I go over to Ben's. It'll be early for Bobby, but he's worn out. It's tough enough on him losing his grandfather all of a sudden without having to put up with Mama slobbering over him, too."

The Wadmans walked Gilly out to the worn-out Ford Dr. Druffitt had passed on to her ages ago, and watched her off down the road.

"Damned shame it couldn't have been Elizabeth instead of Henry," Bert grunted. Back in the kitchen, he headed for the rum again. "After that little episode, I don't know but what I could use another snort. What about you, Jen?"

"That's not such a bad idea. Oh blast! I forgot to turn off the oven. That meatloaf must be like shoe leather."

Janet was sipping at her drink and dishing up the meal when they had yet a third visitor. This time it really was Marion.

"I was wondering if you could spare a pinch of tea. Oh haven't you eaten yet? I thought you'd be finished long ago."

Janet shrugged and began filling the plate she'd meant for Gilly. Bert fixed another tumbler of rum and water without bothering to ask Marion if she wanted it.

"Wasn't that Gilly I saw driving away just now?" The question was purely rhetorical. Marion knew the Wadmans knew she'd been peeking around the curtains over at the Mansion, waiting for Gilly to leave because she didn't quite have the brass to come barging in while her cousin's daughter was still present.

"She came to ask if we'd take Bobby till after the funeral," said Janet. "He'll be here in the morning," she added firmly.

"Now that her old man's gone, I suppose Gilly figured she had to find somebody else she could sponge on fast," said their uninvited guest, holding out her quickly-emptied glass for a refill. "Henry can't have had much to leave her, between the way his practice has been going downhill and his delusions that he knew how to play poker, and you can bet she won't get a cent out of Elizabeth unless she toes the mark. It's high time that little doll-baby learned the facts of life. She's been spoiled rotten since the day she was born."

"I wouldn't say she looked spoiled this evening," said Bert, ignoring the stretched-out tumbler.

"Oh Gilly puts on that 'poor little me' act and everybody falls for it. If she'd had to scratch for a living like I have, she'd know enough to grab what she can get and be damned glad of it. I don't know what she's got to bellyache about. Elizabeth would give her the moon with a pink ribbon tied around it if she'd only ask for it decent."

"If she'd only turn herself into a human doormat, you mean," snapped Janet. "Quit swilling that rotgut and eat your supper, Bert. You'd better get a move on pretty soon, hadn't you?"

Her brother gobbled with an eye on the clock. Marion slowly and deliberately stuffed her long, lean frame as full as possible.

"Jason Bain was up again this afternoon," she remarked between mouthfuls. "He keeps yowling that he'll take me to court unless I give him that patent by Thursday. Can he do that, Bert?"

"How do I know? I'm no lawyer. Save the pie till I get home, eh, Jen."

"Aren't you even going to drink your tea?"

Bert's notable good nature must have cracked at last. He was slamming the kitchen door behind him before Janet got the words out of her mouth. She set the pie back in the fridge, not offering to cut a slice for Marion. At this point, Janet was disliking that woman very much.

Thick-skinned as she was, Miss Emery couldn't help noticing the frost in the air. "That was great, Janet. Thanks a lot. Now I'd better get back and hunt some more before Bain calls out the militia. I don't suppose you'd—"

"No, you needn't suppose anything." The tag end of Janet's endurance was worn clean through. "I've had a rough day and I'm not lifting a hand again tonight."

Janet worked off her spleen on the dishes, then went into the front room and turned on the television. There was nothing worth looking at, but she found relaxation of a sort in lolling back on the chesterfield and gazing through half-shut eyes at the jumping patterns on the screen. Never before, not even that night at the hospital, had she felt so totally drained. Without meaning to, she fell asleep.

When she woke up, everything was pitch black around her except for the television screen. How could she have slept with the volume turned so high? No, the racket was coming from outside. Over at the Mansion a horn was honking, dogs were yapping, people were shouting.

Janet ran to the window. Surely that was her brother's station wagon pulled into the driveway and Bert getting out of it, carrying an armload of something. Clothes, perhaps. Somebody had just switched on an outside light and she could see what looked like a coat sleeve dangling. Whatever could he be doing, and who was that woman with him? Then she saw it was Gilly Bascom with a wiggling bundle in her arms that must be one of the dachshunds. Behind her came young Bobby, also carrying a dog.

Before she'd consciously made up her mind to do so, Janet was out the door and across the yard. "Gilly, what's happened?"

It was the usually taciturn Bobby who answered. "We had a fire! Our house burned up and the goldfish got boiled to death. And Schnitzi had puppies in Mr. Wadman's car!"

"The Owls were breaking up when we spotted the blaze," Bert explained. "Some of us ran and got the engine, but the house was too far gone. We did manage to put up a water screen and save the fire from spreading. Then I brought Gilly and the kid up here. Fred and the rest were still wetting down the ashes when I left."

"I rescued Fritzi," yelled the boy. "Didn't I, Ma?"

"Sure you did, honey," said his mother exhaustedly. "You're a good kid. Look, Marion," her coheiress had appeared with a headful of pink plastic rollers, an old kimono of Mrs. Treadway's clutched about her, "I hate to bust in on you like this, but I couldn't think where else to go."

"The boys' room is all ready," Janet was beginning, but in the face of disaster Marion Emery showed an unexpected streak of benevolence. "Sure, Gilly, why not? This is your house as much as mine. Here, Bert, give me that bundle."

They all trooped in carrying the dachshunds and what few bits and pieces Gilly had managed to snatch from the burning house. Marion eyed the squirming litter of newborn pups with pardonable misgiving. "What do we do with those things?"

"I'm keeping them with me," said Gilly desperately.

"Then you'd better take Auntie's bedroom. It's the biggest. Bobby can have the little room next to it if he wants. I guess we'll have to do something about the beds." Marion obviously wasn't sure what.

Janet stepped in and took charge. "Gilly and I will tend to those. Why don't you nip down to the kitchen and make us all a cup of tea? Bert, you'll find some cartons in the cellar.

Go get one and fix a bed for the pups. There's a bagful of clean dust rags hanging just inside the cellarway."

For a while they were milling around getting in each other's way, finding clean linens, rushing back and forth to the Wadmans' for tea, for milk, for another pair of pajamas to fit Bobby because his were alarmingly scorched around the edges, for a dozen other things. At last they got settled at the kitchen table to eat the pie Janet had saved from suppertime and drink Marion's rather peculiar tea. There was nothing like a catastrophe to bring people together, Janet thought, watching Marion fill Gilly's cup in the friendliest way possible.

"Any idea how the fire got started, Gilly?" Bert was asking.

"All I can think of is that somebody must have thrown a lighted cigarette into that big smoke bush against the front of the house. It's been so dry lately those fuzzy blossoms would have gone up in a flash. I've always known I ought to cut it down, but I never had the heart. It was the only really beautiful thing we had."

She picked at her pie. "Well, that little old cracker box was bound to go sometime. I'm only thankful the fire started at the front instead of the back. Otherwise we might never have gotten out alive."

"I'll bet your mother won't shed any tears when she finds it's gone and you got out all right," said Marion. "She was giving me digs earlier about getting out of here so you and Bobby could move in."

"I'm not surprised. She's been working that line with me ever since Aunt Aggie died. I told her I couldn't possibly manage a place this size even if I were getting money enough out of the estate to keep it up, which I'm sure as heck not. I don't have any intention of driving you out, Marion. I'll find something, somehow."

Her thin shoulders sagged in hopelessness. Her mother's cousin reached over and laid a hand on her arm.

"Forget it, will you? God knows this ark is big enough for both of us. I'll be glad of company, if you want the truth.

Being alone here at night is getting on my nerves. Besides, you can help with the inventory and stuff. Your mother was bending my ear again today about getting the estate settled."

"After Papa died?" gasped Gilly.

"Oh no, before she went to the meeting. I bummed a ride down with Sam Neddick to see if your mother could tell me anything about that patent Bain's been raising the roof over. That was after you ran out on me, Janet," Marion added parenthetically.

"Elizabeth didn't know anything about the patent, but she did manage to get in quite a little speech about the dignity of the family and you having to live in that hovel, as she called it. Then she gave me the bum's rush because she had to get dressed up to put on the dog for that bunch of old hens she hangs out with. I was sort of hoping she'd give me a ride back, but instead I had to hoof it two miles uphill. I was sore as hell at the time, but I sure thanked my lucky stars when I heard about Henry. If I'd hung around a while longer, I might have been the one to find him."

Janet's scalp prickled. So Marion had been down at the Druffitts' before the so-called accident. Maybe she had been the one to find him, and maybe he hadn't been dead until after she'd found him. She could have pretended to leave when Elizabeth went upstairs, then sneaked around through the hedges to the back door, or simply banged the front door and then walked through the waiting room into the office. If she'd been seen around Queen Street afterward, she could always say she'd stopped to shop or something, and if she was a long time getting back to the Mansion, she could have told Dot she'd simply taken her time walking back because it was so hot out.

Marion must have come down from the attic not long after Janet had dropped her bomb in front of Dot and left the Mansion. Dot would surely have been bursting to tell the news, and Marion would have had to be deaf or crazy not to listen. Why hadn't she come over to ask Janet about the find then and there? Why hadn't she brought up the subject at suppertime? She'd been ready enough to talk about other things. Maybe that jar was the one thing she didn't dare mention.

Who but Marion would have every opportunity to fiddle with the jars in the cellar, and who else would be in more urgent need of knowing which were the good beans and which were the bad? She was the likeliest person to be sharing a meal with Mrs. Treadway when they were served. And who else was scatterbrained enough to have forgotten to take away the second jar once the first had done its deadly job? Except Dot Fewter, of course, and Dot was too feckless and too good-natured to plan a murder in the first place.

But Sam Neddick was Dot's very particular friend, so if he was at the Mansion long enough to give Marion a ride, he must also have heard the story of the jar. And Sam had brought Marion down to the Druffitts', where he did chores and knew the layout as well as anybody. And Sam could be the original Invisible Man when he chose. And Sam was a person of dark and devious ways. But why would Sam want to kill Mrs. Treadway, who'd always been so good to him, or Henry Druffitt, with whom he'd remained on friendly enough terms even while he was feuding with Elizabeth?

Suppose, for the sake of argument, Marion Emery's obsession about a cache of money in the Mansion was no mere fantasy. Suppose the reason she hadn't been able to find the cache was that it had already been found? Who was better at finding things than Sam, and who but the man who lived on the premises and did odd jobs in the house would be likelier to come across the cache?

What would Mrs. Treadway do if she learned she'd been robbed? She certainly wouldn't go to Fred Olson; she thought he was about as fit to be marshal as she was to be Prime Minister. She couldn't talk to Bert or Annabelle because there was always the off chance they might either be guilty or think she was accusing them, and she couldn't run the risk of antagonizing her only good neighbors. She'd know better than to breathe a word to Sam or Dot, she'd surely suspect

Marion, she thought Gilly was a flibbertigibbet, she wasn't on speaking terms with Elizabeth.

Henry Druffitt was still her doctor, though, and a doctor was a respectable man. Mrs. Treadway might very well have told her story to Henry. If she had, Sam would have known, because Sam had that mysterious way of finding things out.

And Sam might have thought up that stunt with the jars because he'd know that if she hadn't got around to accusing him yet she would sooner or later, and he might deliberately have left the second one on the shelf after the first had worked so nicely, in the hope that Marion would eat it because Marion was fairly shrewd, too, in her own way, and she was awfully determined about that cache that ought to have been there and wasn't.

Bert brought her out of her disagreeable musings. "Come on, Jen, you're asleep on your feet. Let's get out of here and let these folks go to bed. I daresay we can all use a good night's rest by now."

Nobody needed rest more than Janet, but long after the lights had gone out at the Mansion and Bert's gentle, familiar snore was heard from his and Annabelle's bedroom down the hall, Janet lay awake, wondering which of them did it.

CHAPTER 5

As soon as Janet had fed Bert his breakfast and got him out of the house, she filled a basket with milk, butter, eggs, bacon, and a loaf of the bread she'd baked two days ago. If she knew Marion Emery, there wasn't a bite to eat at the Mansion and if she knew Gilly Bascom, there wasn't a cent to buy anything with. Murderers or not, they had a boy to feed.

Of course, there was always the off chance it was the boy himself who was the murderer. Then again, maybe none of them was. If cold-bloodedness was the prime requisite, Janet would put her own money on Elizabeth Druffitt. Imagine getting at Gilly about where she lived and what she'd live on while her own husband lay stretched out in his coffin! Well, the way things had been going with Henry Druffitt of late, from all reports, maybe his wife didn't count him all that much of a loss. In any case it wasn't for her to judge.

"At least I can stop complaining it's too quiet around here," Janet remarked to the cat as she picked up her basket. None of them would be up yet over there. She'd just slip in and leave the food on the kitchen table, and save Marion the bother of coming over to bum it later.

In fact, Marion was up, still wearing her aunt's kimono and curlers, though by now wisps of that dull-black hair were escaping and straggling down her hollow cheeks. She greeted the donation with open arms.

"Say, this is great of you, Janet! I was just wondering what in hell I could feed those kids."

"I suppose they're still abed."

"No, Gilly's up. She's worried about one of the pups.

We've called the vet and I sure hope he comes soon. Poor little thing, you can't help feeling sorry for it. Bobby's still buzzing away. I peeked in on him before I came down. He looked so cute with that skinny little face, and the other dog tucked in beside him as if it were a teddy bear." Marion smiled, a real, warm, bonafide smile. "Last night he put his arms around my neck and kissed me good night. 'Aunt Marion,' he calls me."

She flushed at this show of softness, and began to unpack the basket. "I bought a pound of coffee yesterday when I was downtown. I'll make some if you'll show me how to work the percolator."

Could this woman possibly be as helpless as she acted? "How do you ever manage when you're by yourself?" Janet couldn't resist asking.

"Use instant. I do know how to boil water, though you mightn't think so. That's what I meant to get yesterday, but they were fresh out."

Janet, feeling silly about doing such a thing with a woman old enough to be her mother, was demonstrating where to put the coffee and where to put the water when the front doorbell rang.

"That'll be the vet," said Marion. "Would you mind letting him in, Janet? I can't go to the door looking like this."

She had a foolproof argument there. Janet stepped into the front hallway. Silhouetted against the stained-glass panels that framed the door, she saw not one but two forms. From the height and lack of breadth, one of them had to be Jason Bain. The other was nearly as tall, and a good deal broader, especially through the chest and shoulders. Janet scuttled back to the kitchen.

"Marion, that's old Bain and I think he's got his son with him. Run upstairs and put your clothes on, quick!"

The bell jangled furiously. "I'd better go let him in before he breaks the door down. Hurry, Marion, I'm not getting stuck with that pair."

Actually she had nothing in particular against Elmer.

About all she could remember of him was that he'd been in Gilly's class at school and was supposed to be a wonderful goalie, only his father would never let him take the time off to play. She didn't think she'd ever spoken two words to him in her life. Nor to old Bain, either, if it came to that. She eased the door open a crack. "Good morning."

The elder Bain wasted no time on pleasantries. "Where's Miz Emery?"

"Upstairs getting dressed."

He took no more notice of Janet, but brushed past her and plunked himself down on the green plush chesterfield with the carved rosewood back. Elmer trailed after his father, looking desperately embarrassed and lugging, for some reason, an old-fashioned cowhide suitcase. Not knowing what else to do, Janet sat down in a chair across the room. Elmer remained standing near the door. He shuffled his enormous boots on the once-red Axminster carpet, cleared his throat several times, and finally, to Janet's amazement, spoke.

"Gilly here?"

His voice was husky as though it never got used much, but not rasping like the old man's. Coming from anybody else it might have sounded rather agreeable. As he was a Bain, Janet felt called upon to resent the question.

"Yes, she's here. Why shouldn't she be?"

The old man snickered. The son ignored him. "Is she all right? She and Bobby didn't get hurt in the fire, eh?"

He sounded as though he honestly cared. Janet began to feel ashamed of herself for being so hostile. "No, they're not hurt, but they lost just about everything, and now one of the puppies is sick."

"Schnitzi's had her pups, then?"

"Yes, in my brother's car on the way up here last night. I guess the excitement was too much for her. Gilly's waiting for the vet now."

"Maybe I could—"

"Set down, Elmer."

Flushing and glowering, the younger Bain obeyed. The

three of them sat in sullen silence until Marion appeared, dressed and with her hair combed. She wasn't wasting any time on small talk, either.

"Look, Mr. Bain, I told you I'd get in touch with you when I find that patent, so why don't you quit bugging me? You know we've had a death in the family."

"I know," he replied. "I'm a reasonable man, Miz Em'ry. I could go down to Fred Olson this minute an' swear out a warrant, but things bein' as they are, I've decided to give you till the end of the week. An' my son Elmer here's goin' to stay an' make sure you don't try to put nothin' over on me."

"What are you talking about?" yelped Marion. "He can't stay here."

"That so? Elmer, you just lug that there grip o' yours upstairs an' find a place to bed down. Go on, move!"

Marion turned to Janet, her face an interesting shade of pale green. "What shall I do?"

Janet shrugged. The only thing she knew against Elmer was that he was a Bain. "Well, I don't know, Marion," she replied cautiously, "if you and Gilly want to take in a boarder, I don't see why you shouldn't. What with the inheritance being tied up and Gilly's getting burned out, people will surely understand that you might need the money."

"What money?" roared the father.

"Yours or his, we don't care which," Janet told him sweetly. "Surely you wouldn't want to start talk around town that your son was being supported by a couple of women? If Elmer wants to pay his share and behave himself, he's welcome enough. If not, as you say, a person could always go down to Fred Olson and swear out a warrant."

Marion stuck out her jaw. "Yeah, that's right. And don't think I wouldn't."

"Now, look here, Paw," stammered Elmer, "I'm not about to stick my nose in where I'm not wanted."

"Who's not wanted?" Gilly had appeared in the doorway, cradling a dachshund in her arms. "Oh hi, Elmer. I thought you were Dr. Bottleby."

"Hi, Gilly. How's the pup?"

"Perking up a little, I think. Come and have a look, eh?"

The pair of them drifted off together. The rest hardly noticed their leaving; they were too busy wrangling over who was going to pay how much to whom. At last the old man wrenched a ten and a twenty off the wad he took from his hip pocket and stamped out, fuming.

"I hope I did right," said Marion, looking nervously down at the serene profile of Her Gracious Majesty on the uppermost bill.

"I don't know what else you could have done, short of calling out the Mounties," Janet replied. "Anyway, at least Elmer's got a car." The Bains must have arrived in separate vehicles, for a tidy-looking Ford was still sitting in front of the Mansion.

"I just hope to God that patent turns up soon," Marion sighed. "What with Bain pestering me and Elizabeth chewing my ear about the estate, I'm ready to fold up. Ah the hell with it. At least we've got grocery money now. Maybe I can get Buffalo Bill there to drive me down to market and back."

"Tell him he'll have to if he expects to be fed. Speaking of food, I've got to get home. That's our last loaf of bread I gave you, and Bert will be in for his dinner before I've even made the beds, at the rate I'm going."

As Janet crossed the yard, a scrap of schoolyard gossip she hadn't thought of for years floated back into her mind. Hadn't Elmer been sweet on Gilly once, and didn't Mrs. Druffitt raise the roof about it? That wasn't so hard to understand. What respectable family would want to get tied up with old Jase? Elmer must take after his mother. Mrs. Bain had died some time ago, probably in order to shuck her husband. She'd been a schoolteacher, as Janet recalled, and some said she'd taken him in desperation, after having given up any other hope of getting "Mrs." on her tombstone.

The Bains must have been awfully old to start a family when Elmer was born. If the father had been in any kind of partnership with Charles Treadway, he must have been a grown young man then; in his twenties, anyway; and that would put him up around seventy now. Why hadn't he laid any sort of claim to this patent before? Even if Mrs. Treadway did hold a lifetime interest in the thing, couldn't he at least have tried to force her to put it into production? What good was a patent unless something was done about it?

Maybe something had been done, and Mrs. Treadway never knew. What if by some miracle Charles Treadway had managed to think up an invention that actually worked, and Bain had been collecting royalties or whatever they called them for years without ever giving the widow her rightful share? What if she'd finally found out, and demanded that he pay what he owed her? Over a span of maybe forty years, even a small annual sum could mount up to a lot of money. Enough to commit murder for, if a person was as attached to his dollars as Jason Bain appeared to be.

Sam Neddick might know, assuming this wasn't all moonshine in the first place. Sam was closer than anybody else in the area to being a crony of Bain's. Sam was clever and Sam was quite possibly buyable. Janet had already faced up to the fact that Sam was as likely a suspect as any when it came to doing the two murders. If he hadn't a reason of his own, would he turn down a good offer from Bain? Who could say?

Marion's decision to stay on at the Mansion after her aunt's funeral must have surprised Sam. He'd no doubt taken it for granted, as the Wadmans had, that she'd either return to her job or at least settle up whatever affairs she might have in Boston before coming back to the Mansion. That would have left him alone here as caretaker, free to rummage for the patent and get it back to Bain. Instead, she'd let everything else drop and stuck to the house like glue. If Sam Neddick was in fact Bain's agent, Marion Emery might very well count herself lucky that he hadn't found a way to get rid of her, too.

CHAPTER 6

The Wadmans were sitting down to a noontime dinner for which Janet had little appetite when Gilly and Elmer came to the back door wanting to borrow Bert's posthole digger. Bobby was tagging behind them.

"How long do you need it for?" Bert asked. "Don't tell me you're planning to dig for the buried treasure?"

Young Bain flushed crimson. Gilly laughed. "Marion's handling that end of the show, thanks. We left her on the phone trying to persuade Mama to come up here after the funeral and help hunt for that idiotic patent of Great-uncle Charles's. I wish Marion would take her up on the roof and shove her off."

"Now, Gilly," said Elmer to everyone's surprise, "that's no way to talk in front of the kid."

"I'm sorry," she replied meekly. "I should know better than to make rotten jokes about people. Shouldn't I, Bobby?"

Gilly was wearing a pair of worn canvas shoes and a stiffly starched cotton housedress that had been her great-aunt's instead of her usual tarty getup. Her face was scrubbed clean of makeup, and her hair was slicked back under a ribbon. Janet hadn't realized she could look so pretty.

"Grandma wouldn't come anyway," the boy piped up. "She says she won't set foot in the Mansion as long as Elmer's here. You're not going, are you, Elmer?"

"Poor Elmer's getting it right and left," Gilly laughed. "Between Mama throwing tantrums over the phone and Marion counting every bite he eats, I'll bet he's sorry he came. Aren't you, Elmer?"

She slid one of her thin hands over the young giant's sleeve and smiled up at him. Elmer looked anything but sorry.

"Elmer thought if you'd lend us the posthole digger for a few hours, we could build a run for the dogs," she explained. "He found a roll of chicken wire out in the barn."

Bain struggled with his Adam's apple for a while, then muttered, "Let 'em run loose and some dern fool Yankee's apt to shoot 'em for deer."

Bert chuckled and went to get the tool. Janet was bringing out the cookie jar for Bobby when yet a fourth visitor arrived. This one was Fred Olson.

"Howdy, folks. What you doin' over here, Elmer? I heard you'd moved into the Mansion."

Elmer stammered something about "Paw's idea."

"How come you ain't workin'?"

"Got a week's holiday."

"Still foreman over at the lumber mill?"

"Yep."

"Goin' to make your million, eh, even if it's only a million toothpicks?"

"Elmer does all right," said Gilly belligerently.

"Never said he didn't. Might as well scratch for yourself, boy. Ol' Jase is bound to figure out some way to take his wad with him when he goes. He give you any idea what that patent's worth?"

"Nope."

"Did he say what it's for?"

"Said I'd know it when I seen it."

"How?"

Elmer shrugged. "Dunno. Ain't seen it yet."

The marshal grunted. "Gilly, how about you tellin' me real careful what happened last night?"

"About what?"

"The fire, o' course. What else?"

"Well, there was that little business of my father, in case you hadn't remembered."

She swallowed hard. "All right, Fred. I didn't mean to be

nasty. I was down at Ben Potts's place with Mama. Visiting hours weren't supposed to be till tonight, but people started dropping in. What with one thing and another, we didn't get out of there till after ten o'clock. I was beat right down to the ground by then, and I guess my mother was, too. Anyway, she went straight along home, and so did I. I just looked in on Bobby to make sure he was all right, then I shucked my clothes and fell into bed.

"I'd already dropped off to sleep when the dogs started kicking up a racket. I thought it might be Schnitzi having her pups, so I jumped up. Then I heard a roaring noise and smelled smoke, and realized the front room was on fire. I ran and woke Bobby and got him and the dogs out of the house, then I think I went in once more to grab a few clothes. I think Bobby started to follow me, but I yelled at him to stay back and get the dogs away from there. He's a good kid," she added defiantly.

"Then what happened?" Olson prompted.

"To tell you the truth, Fred, I can't remember much. I know people were yelling at us to get away from the walls, and there was one great big bang that was probably my car blowing up. The dogs kept yapping and I couldn't seem to think about anything but Schnitzi and her puppies. Then I got soaked with the fire hose and the cold water sort of brought me to my senses. I saw Bert with the firemen, and went over and asked if he'd drive us up to Aunt Aggie's. I—I think I forgot she wouldn't be here any more. Anyway, Marion's been as nice as anybody could want, and Schnitzi had her pups and they're doing fine. Gosh, Bert, I hope she didn't mess up your car's upholstery too much."

"Don't worry, it's plastic," Wadman assured her.

"You got any idea how the fire might have started, Gilly?" the marshal persisted.

"All I can think of is what I said last night: Somebody must have thrown a cigarette or something into the smoke bush out by the front door."

Olson shook his head. "I don't think so, Gilly. Seems to

me I recollect seein' that bush go up in one big puff as we was runnin' toward the house. Can you remember, Bert?"

"Come to think of it, yes I can, a great ball of flame that died right down. I thought it must be the gas tank on the car, but that went later, just before Gilly spoke to me. I remember the bang well enough. So the bush couldn't have had anything to do with it. The fire was already going great guns when we spotted it from the Owls' meeting room."

"Then I don't know what to tell you," said Gilly. "All I know is that it started in the front part of the house, because if it hadn't we wouldn't be standing here now."

"You didn't leave a cigarette burning in the parlor?"

"I couldn't afford to smoke even if I wanted to, which I don't. Anyhow, I was always careful about fire. The place was such a cracker box."

Her voice shook. "I don't think anybody set foot in the front room all evening. Bobby went to bed right after supper, and as I told you, I was over to Ben's with Mama."

"How come your mother never showed up at the fire? I never seen her, an' neither did anybody else I've asked."

"No, that was my one lucky break. She told me over the phone this morning that she'd taken three aspirins as soon as she got home, and slept like a log till I woke her up saying Bobby and I were here with Marion. If she'd known about the fire, she'd have dragged me off to the family tomb while I was still too numb to fight back. Now all she can say is, 'Well, dear, maybe it's worked out for the best.'"

"Maybe it has," said Janet.

That aspect of the matter didn't interest Olson.

"Does the boy smoke?" he barked.

"Not in front of me, he doesn't. I expect he's tried it once or twice, like any boy his age."

"Bobby, was you smokin' or playin' with matches in the house last night after your mother left?"

The boy shook his head.

"I told you he was asleep the whole time," Gilly protested.

The marshal grunted. "You didn't have none o' your chums in?"

"No. I was asleep," the boy repeated doggedly.

"Gilly, you said folks started droppin' in. Anybody come to the house before you left?"

"Only Mama, to make sure I was ready."

"How long did she stay?"

"Only a couple of minutes."

"What did she do?"

"Stood and jawed at me to go wipe off the makeup, and hurry."

"You didn't see nobody hangin' around outside?"

"Not that I can recall. I suppose there must have been somebody or other, there always is. But most of the usuals were over at the Owls' meeting, weren't they?"

"Had close to a 100 per cent turnout," Olson answered with pride in his voice. "How come you never joined the Owls, Elmer?"

"Nobody ever asked me to."

The marshal reddened a little. "Didn't realize you was waitin' for a hand-engraved copperplate invitation. Where was you last evenin', since we're on the subject?"

"Bowlin'."

"Whereabouts?"

"Over to the Fort."

"Who with?"

"Nobody."

"See anyone you knew?"

"Nope. Bunch o' Yanks."

"What time did you get there?"

"Half-past eight, thereabouts."

"How long did you stay?"

"Long enough to bowl four strings an' drink a can o' that bellywash they call beer over there. About eleven, I guess."

"Where was you before that?"

"Home paintin' the house."

"Can you prove it?"

"Go look at the house."

Janet had begun to feel sorry for Fred. What was a country marshal who knew nothing about sophisticated police work supposed to do in a situation like this? Fred knew Gilly's house hadn't burned by accident. Either she'd set it herself, which would have been flirting with suicide and child murder, or else somebody else had, quite likely with the intention of killing both her and Bobby. It was only by the grace of God and the barking of two little dachshunds that they hadn't gone to join Dr. Druffitt.

"Fred," she blurted out, "you've absolutely got to—"

"Thanks," he interrupted loudly, "but I can't stay. Molly's got my dinner all ready an' waitin' on the table, like as not."

The fat old fool! A cold-blooded murderer and arsonist running loose, and all he could think of was his own paunch. Now why was he making faces at her behind everybody else's back? Casually, like any proper hostess, Janet followed him out to the doorstep.

"Janet," he hissed, "can you get down to the shop this afternoon? We got to talk private."

That would teach her to judge not. "That's sweet of Molly," she said aloud. "And tell her how much Annabelle enjoyed all those lovely cards from the Sunshine Circle. She's going to drop a note to the minister's wife when she feels a little more like sitting up. By the way, I might be down to see you myself. The handle on one of our old iron skillets is working loose and I thought maybe you could rivet it or something."

"Why don't you give it to him now, eh, and save yourself a trip?" Bert called out like a typical older brother.

"Because I stuck it away somewhere so I wouldn't make the mistake of using it and dumping your supper on the floor," she lied, "and can't recall offhand where I've put it. What's the sense of keeping Fred standing here missing his dinner while I go hunting? Sit down and eat your own, can't you? It must be ice cold by now."

Gilly took the hint and shepherded her party back to the

Mansion. They made a cute trio, Janet thought, the woman so little and the man so big and the elflike Bobby skipping beside them. She only hoped none of the three had got into the habit of killing people, or was related to someone who had. A person could be guiltless as a newborn babe and still be used as an accomplice, and be charged as one when the case came to trial.

But what if the case did not come to trial? What if the killer was never found? What if he or she or possibly they simply went on living in Pitcherville with nobody the wiser? Would anybody in town be safe then? Wouldn't the murderer feel confident that he could do away with anyone he chose, any time he took the notion?

Janet gave the tea kettle a nervous jerk at the wrong moment, and sent a stream of boiling water coursing across her hand.

"For God's sake, watch what you're doing!"

Bert grabbed his sister's arm, gazing in horror at the rising blisters.

"Let go, Bert. That hurts."

It did more than hurt. The pain was making her sick. Her knees felt wobbly. Janet walked very carefully to the rocking chair by the window and sat down.

"There's some salve in the medicine chest."

That was what she meant to say, but she had trouble forming the words. The next thing she knew, Bert was sloshing at her face with a wet dishrag. She tried to push his hand away.

"Stop it! What are you doing that for?"

"You almost passed out on me. Jesus, what a time for the doctor to die!"

"I'm all right. It was just the shock of it."

It was too many shocks in too short a time, but how was she to explain all that now? Bert was rummaging in the first-aid supplies, bringing ointment and bandage, trying to cover up the burn and making a ham fist of it.

"I'd better get Gilly back here."

"What could she do?"

"How do I know?" He was sweating and yelling, angry at his own helplessness. "She's a doctor's daughter, isn't she? She must know what to do in an emergency."

"Simmer down, Bert. I'm not going to die of a scalded hand. Eat your dinner so you can get back to work."

"You don't expect me to leave you here alone all afternoon? What if you should faint again? You could fall and crack your skull like Doc Druffitt."

That was definitely the wrong thing to say. Janet felt the wave of nausea again, then that wet dishrag slopping her face. Bert scooped her out of the rocking chair, carried her into the front room and plunked her down on the chesterfield.

"Now stay there and don't try to move. I'm going next door and get Gilly or Marion."

"Please don't. They've got more on their hands than they can cope with already, between Gilly's troubles and Elmer's father making all that foofaraw over the patent."

"Then I'll send Sam down for that Fewter woman we had when Annabelle was laid up. She'll be better than nobody."

"Not much," sniffed his sister. "All right, do that if it'll make you feel any better. Tell Dot to plan on staying the night. I'll need help getting my clothes off and on with this bunged-up hand. And be sure to phone Fred Olson and explain why I can't come this afternoon."

"Hell, what difference does that make?"

"Bert, I want Fred told!"

"Well, all right, don't get het up over it. For Christ's sake take it easy till that hand heals over. One sick woman in the family's enough for me."

After he'd gone and it was safe to close her eyes without getting resuscitated, Janet lay still on the couch, trying to rest and think. In a way, she, too, was a victim. If she hadn't been so upset over the murders, she wouldn't have had the accident. That was the way these things went, like weeds getting a foothold in a garden. If they weren't rooted out, they'd spread until they choked out all the good plants and you had nothing left but weeds.

Dot came. Janet got her to help her up to her room and get her clothes off. In a loose nightgown between clean sheets and dosed with aspirin, she felt easier. Having lost so much sleep the night before, she managed to drop off and sleep away the better part of the afternoon. At suppertime she struggled into a housecoat and came down, over Bert's protests.

"For Pete's sake, stop mother-henning me, Bert!" she retorted. "I never got to eat my dinner, and I'm starved."

"Dot could bring you something on a tray."

"No, thanks." She'd already had one of Dot's trays at teatime, and a sloppier mess she never wanted to face.

"Well, then, if you feel up to it." He even went so far as to pull out her chair for her. "Maybe a hot meal would do you good."

Luckily she'd put together a casserole before she hurt herself. Dot had only to warm it up and fix some vegetables for salad. Bert had to rush through supper again since the Owls were to perform some esoteric ritual at the funeral parlor. Thanks to Janet's clumsiness, he'd have to make do with his feathered helmet and his good gray suit instead of his full regalia.

"I hope I can get Elmer Bain to drive over to the cleaner's tomorrow morning and pick up Bert's Owl tunic so he'll have it for the funeral," Janet remarked to Dot after her brother had left. "Elmer's a pretty decent sort, isn't he? I never really got a chance to know him till now."

"Elmer ain't a bad scout, far's I know," Dot agreed with her mouth full. "Kind o' quiet. Them Bains don't waste nothin', not even words. Say, that's a hot one! I got to tell Sam."

"Yes, why don't you?" said Janet. "Elmer doesn't seem to take after his father much, does he?"

"Favors his ma. Miz Bain was a nice enough woman for all she was a McDermott. Gee, no, thanks. If I take one more bite, I'll bust wide open." Dot laid down her fork with obvious regret. "Sam always says you folks set the best table in town. If I was at Miz Druffitt's now, I'd be lucky to get a fried-egg samwitch, an' she'd be countin' how many grains o' sugar I put in my tea."

It would take her a while to count them, Janet thought, the way Dot was ladling it in. How that woman managed to stay so thin on what she ate was another unsolved mystery. Dot was built a good deal like both Elizabeth Druffitt and Marion Emery, now that Janet happened to notice. If the woman would go a little easier on the makeup and do something about her clothes and hair, she might almost pass for another cousin.

Dot rambled on. "Miz Treadway, now, she'd give you all you was o' mind to eat, such as it was. But Miz Druffitt, boy, I can tell you an ant would starve to death in that woman's garbage can. She's got stuff in that house from the year 1, boxes piled up in the attic right to the eaves, and closets full o' clothes she must o' bought thirty years ago, just hangin' there."

It did seem a pity, Janet had to agree, that good stuff should be let go to waste like that when some poor soul—Dot, for instance, no doubt—could be getting the wear out of it. Still she wasn't keen on the idea of sitting here with the hired help gossiping about a woman whose husband was to be buried the next day. She found, though, that Dot was a lot easier to turn on than to shut off.

"She sure is a caution to work for! She'll put on white cotton gloves an' run her fingers over the furniture lookin' for dust." Dot shrugged. "It's no skin off my nose if she wants to ruin a perfectly good pair o' gloves. The doctor wanted to send for one o' them foreign maids once, but Miz Druffitt wouldn't hear of it. They'd have had to board her, see. 'An' besides,' she says, 'she might be pretty and it would cause talk.'"

"Naturally Mrs. Druffitt wouldn't want to cause talk," said Janet. Nobody ever wanted to in Pitcherville, but somehow a lot of people did.

"Oh no, Miz Druffitt's dead set against talk," Dot replied,

not recognizing the irony, as Janet hadn't really expected her to. "That's why she's always at Gilly to move back home. 'What do you think people are saying,' is how she goes on, 'you living like a pauper when you have a lovely home to come back to?' Gilly always gets sore an' says, 'Who the hell cares what anybody says?' so her ma might as well save 'er breath. They've had some rare ol' hairtangles, I c'n tell you."

Dot decided she could manage one more cookie. "Soon as Miz Treadway died, Miz Druffitt started on Gilly to live up here at the Mansion but Gilly wouldn't go for that one, neither. Can't say as I blame 'er there. Ain't it kind of lonesome, bein' stuck up here where there's nothin' to see an' nobody to talk to? At least down in the village there's somethin' doin' all the time, even if it's only Fred Olson fixin' somebody's flat tire."

That reminded Janet of the appointment she'd wanted so desperately to keep. "I hope Sam gave Fred my message," she fretted. "I was going to see him this afternoon."

Dot pounced. "What about?"

Good grief, what had she used for an excuse? Janet racked her brain. "Oh just an old pan I was hoping he could fix. It belonged to my sister-in-law's grandmother."

Dot chewed the last bite of cookie. "You got a fat chance of gettin' any work out o' Fred till after the funeral. He'll be Owlin' all day tomorrow. They're marchin' in solemn procession all the way to the graveyard."

"Yes, I know, and there's that tunic of Bert's to be got. I do rather hate asking Elmer when I barely know him. You don't suppose Sam could take a run over first thing in the morning?"

"I don't see how. Soon as he finishes his chores here, Sam's got to get slicked up an' go help Ben Potts."

"Then it's Elmer or nobody. I can't possibly drive one-handed all that way and Bert won't have time. Is he at the Mansion now, I wonder?"

Dot applied a well-schooled eye to the edge of the curtain.

"Yep. Leastways his car's in the yard. You'd o' thought he'd be down at the funeral parlor with everybody else."

"Why should he?" said Janet. "The Bains and the Druffitts have never been all that chummy, have they?"

"You c'n say that again! Say, you should o' been a fly on the wall that time Elmer ast Gilly to the high-school dance. I thought Miz Druffitt would throw a fit. No daughter of hers was goin' to be caught out in public with no Bain, she says. So then Elmer got up on his high horse an' says to Gilly if he wasn't good enough for 'er folks he wouldn't ast 'er no more."

"How did you happen to hear that?"

"Oh I heard," said Dot airily. "So the next thing anybody knew she'd run off an' married that no-good Bob Bascom an' if that ain't cuttin' off your nose to spite your face, I'd like to know what is."

"Gilly's had a rough time of it," Janet sighed.

"Don't talk to me about rough times. I got no sympathy to spare for anybody that don't know which side their bread's buttered on."

Dot sounded so exactly like Marion Emery that Janet blinked. Maybe there was some private reason why Mrs. Treadway and Mrs. Druffitt had continued to tolerate the woman's slapdash ways for all their complaints. Maybe the reason wasn't so private, just stale gossip that nobody had ever got around to telling young Janet Wadman. Well, what difference did it make?

"Want me to run over an' ast Elmer about gettin' that tunic?" Dot was offering, eager to be up and doing now that she'd eaten everything in sight.

"Yes, I'd appreciate that." Janet had had about all she could stand of Dot Fewter for a while. "You can wash the dishes," she added firmly, "when you come back. I'm going up to bed."

CHAPTER 7

Henry Druffitt had not been the warmhearted old country GP beloved of sentimental novelists. He'd been punctilious about collecting his bills, when he had any to collect, and caustic with patients who waited till after the late movie on television to demand house calls. However, he had been a life-long resident, a leading citizen of sorts, and a prominent Owl. Pitcherville turned out in force to give him a grand sendoff.

The Wadmans were doing their bit along with the rest. Bert was marching in full Owl regalia, Elmer having been most co-operative about the dry cleaning. Janet, feeling very lady-of-the-manor, had spent half the morning out in the garden showing Dot which blossoms to cut for the church, and sent them down by Sam when he made one of his mysterious trips back to the hill.

She dropped over to make sure the group from the Mansion got something to eat before they left, and found them already dressed for the funeral, self-consciously elegant in newly purchased mourning clothes, except for Elmer, who wasn't to be included in their party. Mrs. Druffitt was having Potts send up a special car for them.

"Mama wants us down there early," Gilly told Janet, "so she can get us bawling good. She thinks it'll make a better impression going up the aisle."

"Now, Gilly," said Elmer, "you shouldn't talk that way in front of the kid."

Marion went so far as to thank Janet for her thoughtfulness and wish she could sit with them in church. That, of course, would not be possible. Rigid protocol was being observed.

In the end, Janet rode down with Elmer and Dot Fewter, since Bert had to go on ahead to form up with the Owls. When they got there, Dot cavorted away to join a livelier group. The other two were ushered to a seat of no importance near the back.

Though this was supposed to be a sad occasion, the church had a festive air about it. Outside its high palladian windows, trees made patriotic maple-leaf patterns against a sapphire sky. The altar was ablaze with zinnias, marigolds, gaillardia, splashing their wild reds and yellows against the gentler shades of cosmos and lupine.

Many children were present, gay as the flowers in resurrected Easter finery. Why not? What if they'd come only because they'd begun to find the long summer holiday hanging heavy on their hands and wanted to see the Owls march in? Let them experience a funeral as a sort of celebration, Janet thought, one that was solemn yet somehow comical, a death that was really a birth.

The Owls looked no more outlandish in their feathered regalia than some of the rest in their go-to-meeting clothes. There was old Mrs. Nurstead in the Empress Eugenie hat she'd bought to greet the then Prince of Wales back in 1932. There was Malcolm Webb in the bright green suit he always wore to weddings and funerals, a red bandanna handkerchief peeping modishly out of the breast pocket. There was Bill Hendricks wearing his World War II uniform, not wanting anybody to forget he'd been a sergeant major, as if anybody could. There was Mrs. Fewter looking like the leftovers from a rummage sale.

Dot Fewter had gotten herself up regardless for the occasion, in a dashing black velvet hat somebody must have given her and a black satin dress with a rhinestone dagger plunging dangerously down the bosom. Her costume accentuated the likeness to Marion and Elizabeth that Janet had noticed the night before. No doubt some of the older village gossips could explain the coincidence, if she'd been interested enough to ask.

This was no time to be thinking of such things. Janet folded her right hand over the fresh bandage on her left and stared down at her demure gray-and-white polka-dot lap. She ought to be meditating about Dr. Druffitt, quietly and reverently as befitted the occasion and the place. All she could think about was that he ought not to be dead.

Who beside herself knew that? Fred Olson did, but he wasn't here yet. He was out front, no doubt, ready to march in with the Owls. And the killer, where was he, or she? Sitting here in one of these hard pews, pulling a long face? Somewhere far away, laughing at the farce that was being played out here today? Or standing in the vestibule clad in new black mourning garb, crying so it would look better going up the aisle?

The organ began to play. The minister entered, his black robe dingy and somber against the glory of the flowers. The Owls marched in, six of them carrying the coffin, the rest keeping the slow, even step they'd been practicing down at their meeting room. Every face was grave under its fluffy, speckled helmet, every eye fixed on the altar.

Bert looked as well as any and better than most. Fred Olson's tunic was strained too tight over his middle-aged paunch. He'd be lucky to get through the funeral without popping a seam. What was the man doing here anyway, parading around in a silly costume when he ought to be out tracking down the killer?

Janet's burst of fury died down as quickly as it had swept over her. Lord pity him, Fred was no more a policeman than she was. He'd married late and made up for lost time, still had three kids in school. How could he afford to be high-minded about risking his position in the village?

The mourners were filing in now: Mrs. Druffitt on the arm of Ben Potts, heavily draped in black, her spine stiff, her face blankly pallid; Gilly clutching Bobby's hand, both of them looking small and scared and lost; Marion sharp and pinched but with a city-smart air about her new black suit. Mrs. Druffitt had paid for all the mourning clothes, even Marion's.

Several out-of-town Druffitts followed, all wearing black bands around their sleeves. It was being whispered about the church that one brother had flown all the way from Vancouver.

Dr. Druffitt got a long service. The minister seldom had the chance to preach to an overflowing church, and Janet couldn't blame him for making the most of his opportunity. But her hand was smarting and she still felt wobbly. She was immensely relieved when the Owls finally marched back down the center aisle with their mournful burden and the congregation was free to straggle out of the pews.

This, too, was done according to protocol, front rows first. It was some time before Janet and Elmer could work their way to the door. In the vestibule, Mrs. Druffitt and her entourage stood having their hands squeezed by a seemingly endless line of sympathizers. Janet, almost at the tail end of the procession, made her condolences as brief as possible. She was uncomfortably aware of people nudging each other and hissing, "There's Janet Wadman, the one who found him."

Elmer, behind her, had got no farther than, "Gilly, I—" when Mrs. Druffitt cut in.

"Come, Gillian, we must get out to the car."

Deliberately, she turned her back on young Bain, taking her daughter by the arm and forcing Gilly to do the same. Elmer turned dull red. Quickly, Janet touched his sleeve.

"Could you get me home quick, Elmer? I think I'm going to faint."

"Eh? Oh sure. Glad to. Maybe you better stay here and I'll bring the car around."

He was pathetically eager to help, to reassure himself that he was good enough for somebody.

"No, please don't leave me alone in this mob. I can walk, if you'll give me a hand going down the stairs. My word, Elmer, I don't know what we'd all do without you."

She was laying it on thick, trying to get the hurt look off his face. A man that size had no business being so vulnerable.

"Some folks can do without me fine," he muttered.

"Don't take any notice."

That was stupid, but what else could she say?

They were in his car and halfway up the hill road before he let himself explode.

"That old bitch! I'm sorry, Janet, but—"

"Don't apologize. I was trying to think of something stronger, myself, but I don't know any words bad enough. How any woman could stoop to such a trick at her own husband's funeral is beyond me!"

They fumed in companionable silence for a hundred feet or so, then Elmer broke out again.

"I don't know what she's got against me. I always tried to act decent in front of her, but she never gave me a chance. Can I help it if my name's Bain?"

"Of course not!"

"Gilly an' me," a wistful smile curved his lips, "I always liked her, even when we was little kids. I 'member pushin' her on the swing at recess. She was skinny an' big-eyed then like she is now. She don't change none. Neither do I, I s'pose."

His jaw set harder. "I'd have stood up to the Druffitts if it wasn't for Paw. He was all for me grabbin' Gilly because she'd be comin' into money someday. That night I went to ask her to the high-school dance, her mother accused me of fortune-huntin' and what could I say, with Paw shootin' his mouth off like that? I lit out from there right then an' said I'd never go back. Then Gilly run off with Bob Bascom that wasn't worth the powder to blow him to hell, and I—ah, what's the sense rakin' it up again? What I should o' done was take Gilly an' go out West somewheres, away from the whole damned lot of 'em."

"Well, Elmer, you're both still young people."

That was probably more than she ought to have said. It was getting so Janet didn't dare open her mouth. Elmer wouldn't need much coaxing right now to do what he probably should have done years ago, which might be wonderful for him and Gilly and Bobby if all three were what they appeared to be. But were they?

Neither he nor his childhood sweetheart had shown any prodigious amount of backbone so far, when you came right down to it. Maybe it was pride that had driven Elmer away from the girl he loved, but would a stronger man have let himself be driven? He was still living with his father, perhaps because he felt that being a Bain made him too much of a pariah to live anywhere else, but why had he been willing to settle for such a fate?

Wasn't she being a touch overcritical for someone who'd come pretty darn close to making the same mistake Gilly Druffitt had? Instead of moaning over Roy, she ought to be thanking her stars she'd got free of him with nothing worse than a scar on her tum and a punctured balloon.

As for Gilly, what was to become of her? Together, she and Elmer might scrape up strength enough for a successful match. Apart, what had they done? Was it fair for Janet Wadman to judge? Was it even safe to wonder?

Rounding the crest of the hill, they could descry a vehicle parked in front of the Mansion. "That's funny," Janet remarked, "you'd think everybody would know they're down at the funeral."

"He'd know," said Elmer.

The venom in his tone startled Janet. Then she realized she was looking at Jason Bain's old truck. Elmer shoved his foot down on the gas pedal and gunned toward the Mansion in a spray of gravel. Not even pausing to shut the car door after him, he rushed up the steps and slammed into the house.

"You derned old snake," Janet heard him yell, "what are you up to now?"

The father's reply was inaudible. Elmer's was anything but. "Get the hell out of here before I knock your goddamn block off!"

If Elmer Bain was staging a scene for Janet Wadman's benefit, then a great talent was being wasted at the lumber mill. She was wondering if she'd better go in there and try to stave off a third murder when Jason Bain stormed out the door.

"You're no son o' mine," he was roaring.

"I wish I could believe that!" Elmer yelled after him.

"You'll never get your hands on one red cent!"

"You can take your money and shove it up your—"

Elmer's closing words were, perhaps fortunately, drowned out by the noise of old Bain's motor. The truck charged furiously over the hill. The son glared after it, his face contorted as if he needed to vomit. As Janet walked up to join him, he shook his head. "Can't blame the woman. Who in hell would want her daughter to get tied up to a thing like that?"

"What was he doing in the house?" Janet asked.

"How should I know? Claimed he was lookin' for that goddamned patent. Said he had a right to what was his. Cussed old crook! If he had his rights, he'd o' been hung long ago."

Again Janet felt an impulse to comfort the stricken giant. "Now, Elmer, maybe you're being too hard on your father. Marion hasn't been able to find any sign of those papers yet, and he does seem quite desperate to get hold of them. Maybe the time limit's about to expire or something. He never gave you any inkling of what it's all about?"

"Never told me nothin'. Just sat there smirkin' like a jeezledy crocodile, pattin' himself on the back about how you got to be smarter than the next one to get on in this world. Where's he ever got that's so almighty wonderful? Answer me that one."

Since the question was obviously rhetorical, Janet didn't try. "I tell you what, Elmer: Let's you and I have a look for that patent right now. Once it's found, your father won't have an excuse to come bothering Gilly any more. You start hunting. I'll just run over and change my dress, then come back and give you a hand."

Since she had but the one hand to give, she wouldn't be of much use, except to give moral support while Elmer worked off his mad. And to keep an eye out just in case the son did happen to stumble on the patent and turn out to have a streak of old Bain in him after all.

CHAPTER 8

Janet was trying to get her good dress off without hitting her sore hand when Dot Fewter telephoned, wanting to know if Janet could spare her that night. Some of the out-of-town relatives were staying over, and Mrs. Druffitt was begging her to help out.

"Yes, of course," Janet replied with secret relief. "I can manage."

"Okay if you say so, but I was sure lookin' forward to supper at your house."

Well, life held its disappointments for everyone. Janet hung up, slipped her feet into moccasins, managed to get a wraparound housedress of Annabelle's over her bandage, and sauntered into the yard, not hurrying to shut herself away in that dismal old Mansion out of the sun and the air.

What was she doing it for, anyway? Two days ago Elmer Bain was just somebody she vaguely knew as she vaguely knew everybody in Pitcherville with whom she'd never had occasion for any personal dealings. Now she was pretending she didn't have a splitting headache and a terribly sore hand so that she could be with him, not that she had any great fondness for him as a man, but just because he was big and clumsy and hurt, and had a rotten father, and was in love with a girl she'd gone to Sunday school with, a frightened wisp who might be a murderess, or the mother of one.

Judging from the crashes that greeted her entrance, Elmer was in the process of smashing a complete dinner service for twenty-four. Janet reached the pantry just in time to watch a gigantic tureen slide to the floor and splinter.

"Barely leaned against the shelves and the whole dern thing came tumblin' down on me," he muttered.

"Nobody's going to hate you for that," she reassured him. "That was the ugliest set of dishes ever made. Mrs. Treadway had them wished on her as a wedding present and she hated them till the day she died. She used to tell me she prayed for an earthquake, so maybe you've just fulfilled a dying prayer." Deliberately, Janet picked up a saucer that had somehow escaped the holocaust and flung it into the pile of shards. "Go find a dustpan and a garbage can. If it'll ease your conscience, you can buy Marion and Gilly another."

She stirred the debris with the toe of her moccasin, turned up another whole saucer, and smashed that, too. Elmer must think she'd gone crazy with the heat, but she found the crashing of china a great way to relieve tension. Her nerves must be in even worse shape than she'd thought they were. Maybe she'd better simmer down.

"I'll leave you the joy of cleaning up. I think I'll go take a look in the library."

"Marion spent most of yesterday in there," he pointed out as he sloshed a dustpan full of broken dishes into the can.

"Yes, but she may have missed something. Mrs. Treadway told me that was where her husband worked out his inventions mostly, so it seems reasonable he'd keep his patents there." Furthermore, the room was one Mrs. Treadway herself had never used. Janet could be in it without having to feel how empty the house seemed without her old friend's presence.

She was sure it would be a waste of time to search the desk, and it was. Marion's fingerprints even appeared on the dusty wooden runners that held the drawers in place. Janet wasn't about to start prying for loose floorboards and secret panels; Marion would have done that, too. Then what was left? The books, of course. All the Treadways had been great readers, the stacks were crammed to the high ceiling, and so far as she could see the dust on them hadn't been disturbed. Marion must have been too cowed by their numbers to tackle what was surely the most obvious place to search. Janet began to feel the thrill of the hunt.

"Let's see," she mused, "a person would be most apt to take a book from somewhere around eye level. But I'm only five-foot-three and I think Mr. Treadway was quite tall, so— oh gosh." Trying to unravel the thought processes of a man who'd invented an automobile that ran by clockwork and had to be rewound every hundred feet wasn't going to get her far. She dragged a chair over and sat down to check whatever book she could reach simply because that was easiest.

"Hey, look what I found!" Elmer's jubilant yell startled her so that she almost fell off the chair.

"Is it the patent?"

"Gorry, no." He loomed in the doorway, holding up a dusty bottle filled with a dark red fluid. "It's a secret cache of old Mr. Treadway's homemade cherry brandy. Boys oh girls, if Paw knew there was a swig of this stuff left in the house, I'd never of got 'im out. Only time I ever seen tears in his eyes was when he told me old man Treadway carried the secret of makin' it to his grave. Must be ten or a dozen bottles hid behind a loose board in the bottom cupboard right out there in that pantry."

"Mrs. Treadway was death on liquor. He wouldn't have wanted her to find it, and I guess she never did." Janet felt a bit teary-eyed, too. "Imagine, after all those years!"

"Must be pretty potent by now." The young giant fiddled with the cork, his blue eyes filled with wistful longing.

"Go ahead, open it if you want to," said Janet. "You're the one who found it."

He hesitated, then plunked the bottle down on Charles Treadway's desk. "No. I won't take nothin' that's not mine."

"Suit yourself."

Janet went back to pulling out books. She was hot and sticky and choking with dust. Her hand was throbbing worse by the minute. She was sick and tired of the Mansion and all its problems, Elmer Bain's included.

"This is positively the last."

She wrenched one final volume off the shelf. A yellowed envelope spiraled to the floor. She picked it up and saw the words, "Patent Office" in the corner. She glanced at the title of the book in her hand. It was Mary Webb's *Precious Bane.* How dumb could a person get?

Janet didn't realize she'd asked that question out loud till she heard Elmer call, "You talkin' to me?"

"No, just cussing myself out for a blind fool. You can quit hunting, Elmer. I think I've found it."

Elmer came in and compared the envelope and the book title, scratching his blond curls with a remarkably dirty paw.

"Well, I'll be derned! How do you suppose Marion missed seein' that?"

"No doubt she was too busy looking for secret panels in the woodwork. If I'd had my wits about me, I might have noticed it myself before getting covered from head to foot with dust and cobwebs. Anyway, I've done my bit and good luck to 'em. Now I'm going home and lie down. This hand is killing me."

"Gosh, Janet, I forgot you wasn't feelin' good. Want me to walk you over?"

"Thanks, but I'm not that far gone." Janet laid the envelope on the desk beside the brandy. "Give this to Gilly or Marion, whichever gets here first."

Elmer backed away. "I don't want no part of that thing. What if some of the papers are missin'? Gilly's mother'll say I took 'em."

"Oh for the love of Pete!" Janet grabbed the patent and stuffed it in the pocket of her wrapper. "That makes me the goat, as usual. Tell them if they want it, they can come and get it."

"Janet, I'm sorry." Bain did look wretched.

"All right, Elmer. I understand how you feel. I'll just be glad when this foolishness is settled." If it ever was. Somehow, Janet hadn't much faith in *Precious Bane.*

She went over home, peeled off her filthy wrapper and underwear, and took a long shower, soaking her bandage in the process. Bert or somebody would have to help her put on a fresh dressing. No matter; it was worth a little blood poisoning to feel clean again. She put on a change of underclothes and her rosebud wrapper, and stretched out on the bed.

Lying down made her head pound all the worse. "Seems to me I've had a splitting headache ever since I found that cussed jar," she sighed to the cat, who had made himself comfortable on the edge of her robe, always ready to share anybody's catnap. "I'd better ask Bert to pick up another jar of aspirin when he's downtown. Julius, where's it going to end?"

The cat lolled over on his back and stretched out a plush-covered paw. He didn't give a hoot one way or the other. She'd been lying there a fair while, scratching his stomach and wishing she could share his mood, when Marion Emery blew in.

"Where is it, quick?"

"Right over there on the dresser."

"What does it say?"

"How should I know? I'm not in the habit of prying into other people's private business any more than I have to."

Marion was too busy tearing at the tough, yellowed envelope to listen. With a hand that trembled, she tugged out a sheaf of legal-looking paper. "This is it, all right. Treadway Enterprises Ltd, Charles Percival Treadway and Jason Asaph Bain, principals. Patent for—" she flipped through the pages. "What the hell? Janet, does this make sense to you?"

"Quit flapping those papers around and maybe I'll be able to see." In spite of her headache, Janet sat up and steadied Marion's flying hands so that she could get a look at the patent. "Hold it up so I can—oh Marion, this is ridiculous! A self-emptying washtub. Hadn't the old fool ever heard of washing machines?"

"Wait a second! How could they have washing machines up here before they ever had electricity?"

"You turned it with a crank, of course. I could show you a better one than that in any old mail-order catalog. If you want my frank opinion, that patent isn't worth the paper it's written on."

"But it has to be," Marion sounded both pugnacious and worried. "Why would Bain be in such a swivet to get his claws on it if it wasn't? And if he thinks he can swindle me out of my fair share, he's got rocks in his head."

"I wouldn't get my hopes up too high if I were you, eh?"

"Thanks, pal." Marion kept on fluttering pages, her thin face avid. "Okay, so maybe it's not the washtub itself, maybe it's something to do with the principle it works on. I'll bet Bain's seen some new product that infringes on this mechanism, and he figures on holding up the manufacturer for a healthy cut of the profits. He'd need this for evidence, wouldn't he?"

"You mean this particular set of plans? I don't see why. They must keep copies of patents in Ottawa or somewhere. Couldn't he have written away for one? Anyway, I can't see where there's any great mechanism involved. It looks to me like a plain old wooden washtub hooked on to a ratchet thing, like an automobile jack."

"Since when have you been an expert?" snarled Marion. "Let me handle this, will you?"

"Gladly."

Even Marion couldn't miss the ice in Janet's voice. "Look, I didn't mean to get you sore. It's just that you haven't had as much business experience as I have. You don't know how those big corporations operate."

"No, and I can't say I much care." Janet only wished Marion would take herself and her precious documents elsewhere.

However, the heiress showed no sign of leaving. She spread the pages out on the bed, annoying the cat Julius, who flounced off in a huff, and stood frowning over them importantly. "I suppose I'll have to show Gilly. She'll probably start yapping that we've got to turn this right over to Elmer."

"He wouldn't take it," said Janet wearily.

"Don't kid yourself, sister. This is what he came for, isn't it?" Marion shuffled the pages back together and folded them into the torn envelope. "Well, I don't suppose there's much more I can do today. Gilly'll be down at Elizabeth's till God knows when. They've got a pack of Henry's relations hanging around to see if there'll be any pickings for them. That's a laugh. I'll bet you anything you like that Henry even cashed in his life insurance and gambled that away. Even if there is anything, I'd like to see anybody pry a cent away from Elizabeth. I think I'll show this to her first instead of Gilly. At least she's got a head on her shoulders. In the meantime, I'd better go put this away someplace where it'll be safe."

"Yes, why don't you?" said Janet with the first enthusiasm she'd been able to muster. "Pin it inside your roll-on."*

She finally managed to get rid of Marion. Julius immediately hopped back up on the bed and she resumed their conversation.

"Big corporation, my left foot! Julius, what am I supposed to think now? Whatever Mrs. Treadway and Dr. Druffitt were killed for, it certainly couldn't have been over any patent washtub. Or could it? Is it possible there's something more to those papers than we could see? Did I make a mistake letting Marion take them back to the Mansion without warning her there's a murderer on the loose?"

But did Marion need to be warned? Marion was a far likelier suspect than she was a victim, and Janet Wadman had already stuck her neck out far enough to be dangerous to somebody. Everybody in town knew she'd been the one to find Dr. Druffitt's body, after all that buzzing down at the funeral. Thanks to Dot Fewter and her mother, they must also know how she'd happened to be on the spot.

Could she even trust Fred Olson not to betray what she'd observed about that dent in the dead man's skull? He was probably down at the Owls' right now with a few wallops of rye under his belt, dropping a hint in strictest confidence to six or eight of his cronies. And the brother Owls would pass the word to their wives, and the wives to their best friends,

* Note to U.S. readers: Janet was talking about a girdle, not a deodorant.

and before long somebody would put two and two together and come up with yet another minus one.

When Bert got home a few minutes later, he found her in the bathroom vomiting. She wiped her face on a wet washrag and stood holding on to the sink, shaking and sweating. "I guess I did too much today. I'm all right now."

"You sure as hell don't look it."

Her brother sounded frightened, and no wonder. The face in the mirror was enough to scare anybody. Her skin looked pale green, her eyes like a couple of overripe plums.

"Bert, I—" she swallowed what she'd been about to say. What good would it do to tell her brother everything? He'd be better off not knowing. So would she, but it was too late to think about that now.

CHAPTER 9

Janet passed a wretched night. Bert wanted her to stay in bed the next morning, but she insisted on getting up. "I'd go crazy just lying there," she told him.

She really would. It was going to be some job convincing Bert that she was well enough to drive the car down to the village by herself, but she must. Somehow or other, she had to see Fred Olson, alone.

For once, luck was with her. She was slopping around trying to do up the breakfast dishes with one hand when the marshal poked his head in through the back door.

"Bert around?"

"Oh Fred, thank God! No, Bert's out back somewhere."

"Good." He came in and shut the door behind him. "You told him yet?"

"No, I haven't breathed a word to a soul. I'm scared to, if you want the truth."

He nodded, his pudding face creased with down-pulled lines. "Me too. Cripes, Janet, I can't even think straight."

"Here, Fred, sit down." She got him a mug of tea and slid a plate of doughnuts across the table. "I'm afraid they're kind of stale. I scalded my hand day before yesterday and haven't been able to do much."

"That's all right. I'm kind of off my feed, anyway. Molly says she never thought she'd live to see the day." Olson snorted. "She keeps askin' what ails me. What am I s'posed to tell 'er? She'd either have me carted off to the booby hatch or pass the word without meanin' to and get the whole dern village down on me like hawks on a hen roost. God a'mighty, if I could just get my grubhooks on one real piece of evidence!"

"I suppose you've gone over Gilly's house?" Janet suggested. "You couldn't find any sign the fire might have been set?"

"Hell's flames, there wasn't enough left o' that place to put in your left eyeball. I stomped around in the ashes till I was black as the ace o' spades an' all I got out of it was another jawin' from Molly. Ol' wooden crackerbox with the wirin' frayed worse'n a country parson's shirt cuffs an' nothin' but them kerosene room-stinkers for heat, it's a wonder the house didn't burn long ago. Only it didn't. It burned that same night Hank Druffitt was killed, an' his daughter an' his grandson damn near went up along with it. An' that's one coincidence more'n I can swallow."

He took a swig of the cooling tea, set the thick white crockery mug down on the red-checked tablecloth, and stared into its milky dregs. Janet gave him another prod.

"What did the doctor say about that hole in Dr. Druffitt's skull?"

"Said it was a fracture o' the cranium."

"Well, that's a big help, I must say! We could have told him that ourselves. Didn't he say anything else?"

"Said it must o' killed 'im instant, which ain't much help neither."

"But what about the shape of the break? Didn't you ask him?"

"To tell the truth, I never got a chance," Olson admitted. "Elizabeth was there by the time he come with his daughter drivin' an' she was takin' on somethin' awful about how it was all her fault for leavin' that rug there where a person could slip on it an' she should o' known better, which was no more than God's honest truth, I must say, an' she was blamin' herself an' gettin' more an' more worked up till he had to take 'er in on the sofa an' give 'er somethin' to calm 'er down an' by the time he'd done that his daughter was all hot an' bothered about him overstrainin' himself an' she hauled 'im off home an' there I was. An' just about then Ben Potts come along an' by then Elizabeth was a little more like herself only she had to keep dabbin' at 'er eyes with one o' them fancy little han'kerchiefs the size of a postage stamp like she always carries, an' they got to talkin' about the funeral so I figured I might as well pull out an' leave 'em to it."

"Didn't you ask Ben Potts?" Janet persisted. "What did he think?"

"Yep, I asked 'im later on when I got 'im alone. Ben looked me square in the eyes an' says, 'Fred, I never think. I just do what my customers tell me to,' an' you can make o' that anything you please, but if I know Ben that's all you'll ever get out of 'im."

"I suppose it's no more nor less than you might expect," Janet admitted. "What he meant was that Mrs. Druffitt would scalp him with a dull knife if he started any talk."

"Damn it, Janet, can you blame the man? If Elizabeth was to find fault with the way Ben handled the funeral an' decide to send for an undertaker from somewheres else, you know what would happen to him. Same thing as happened to Hank, only worse. At least Hank still got the odd jobs like bandagin' sprains an' takin' fishhooks out o' kids' fingers, but an undertaker only gets one crack per customer."

"No, I'm not blaming him, Fred, and I'm not blaming you, either. The only person I blame is myself, for shooting my mouth off when I should have kept quiet, but that's water over the dam now. What really matters," Janet wiped her good hand across her haggard face, "is that we've still got a killer loose in this town, and I've got a hunch Ben's next customer is going to be me."

Olson started to say, "How do you figure that?" then he stopped short. "Jee-hosaphat! If he was to get wind of you knowin'—"

"He has to know already, doesn't he?" Now that the issue was out in the open, Janet found she could speak quite matter-of-factly. "By the time I got down there with that jar of green beans, Dot Fewter must already have started broadcasting the fact that I'd found it and taken it to show the doctor. We've already agreed Dr. Druffitt must have been killed to keep him from comparing that jar with the one that killed Mrs. Treadway, haven't we?"

"I s'pose so," Olson mumbled.

"And Mrs. Druffitt told me when I met her at the door that she thought she'd heard the doctor come home a few minutes before while she was upstairs. So that means he must have been killed just about the same time I walked into the waiting room, doesn't it? How does the person who killed him know I didn't see something I wasn't supposed to?"

"Gorry, Janet, you could o' been killed yourself, right then an' there."

"Yes, I could, though even Ben Potts mightn't have been willing to swallow two accidental deaths in the same house at the same time. I figure the only thing that's saved me so far is that the killer doesn't know whether or not I believe Dr. Druffitt really slipped on that rug. Once he finds out I don't, then I'm a dead duck. And I'm afraid you are, too. I'm sorry, Fred."

Olson shoved away his mug and got up. "All right, Janet. Guess it's time we called in the Mounties."

CHAPTER 10

Everybody knows what a Royal Canadian Mounted Policeman looks like. He is lean, bronzed, straight-backed, steel-
jawed, handsome as all getout, and stands six-foot-four in his
socks. He wears a dashing red tunic, shiny boots, and blue
jodhpurs with yellow stripes up the sides. Mounties are most
apt to be found either astride magnificent stallions, singing,
"Rose Marie, I Love You," or else driving strings of huskies
across frozen wastes of snow with the aurora borealis flashing
behind them and repentant renegades lashed to their sleds.

Janet Wadman had no trouble whatever passing off Detective Inspector Madoc Rhys of the RCMP as Annabelle's
cousin from Winnipeg. He looked like an unemployed plumb-
er's helper. After a short but surprisingly reassuring interview, she left him to study the family album for background,
and stepped across to the Mansion.

"I don't know what to do, Marion. Bert and I never even
knew the Duprees had any Welsh relatives till this Cousin
Madoc appeared on the doorstep with his suitcase in his
hand. And there's Annabelle in hospital and here's me laid up
with this hand."

"Couldn't you shove him off on Annabelle's folks?" was
Marion's kindhearted suggestion.

"I don't know I'd care to do that. The Duprees already
have the kids to cope with. Anyway," Janet lowered her voice
and glanced around though she knew perfectly well nobody
was there to overhear, "I called up Aunt Maggie on the sly
while he was washing up, and she says Madoc's a bachelor
with pots of money, though I must say you'd never know it to

look at him. Besides, all Annabelle's brothers and sisters are down there and—well, you know Annabelle's not the sort to expect a handout from anybody but you also know the problems she and Bert have been having lately. I wouldn't want to—"

"Sure, I understand." To Marion, nothing could appear more natural than the urge to butter up a rich relative, even if he didn't happen to be hers. "Say, I'll tell you what: Why don't you send him over here to sleep till your hand heals?"

Janet was not at all surprised by the offer, though she pretended to be. "Do you really mean it? It would be heaven if I didn't have to make his bed and pick up after him. That's the one thing that really bothers me. I can manage the meals all right."

She'd have to. There was probably some government law against feeding a Mountie the kind of food Marion Emery cooked. However, he'd have to decide for himself whether to face that peril. Her orders had been, "Just get me into the Treadway house without letting anybody know who I am. I'll carry on from there."

She presumed he'd be able to. Janet had been grateful when Fred Olson came back and told her the RCMP were sending a plainclothes man, but she hadn't expected one quite this plain.

Detective Inspector Rhys knew what she was thinking as he sat back at his newly adopted cousin's house turning over the pages of the family album and memorizing enough names for plausible conversation. It was what people always thought. Not yet thirty years of age, Rhys had already faced mad trappers, salmon poachers, alien smugglers, rioters, ax murderers, and irate wives. He had tracked down snipers, airplane hijackers, foreign spies, and illegal parkers. He had survived blizzards, black flies, stabbings, shootings, and being hit over the head with an electric guitar in a Moncton restaurant.

Through all these adventures, he had remained a sad-faced wisp of a Welshman, barely the minimum five feet, eight inches in height and so thin you had to look at him twice to make sure he was really there. He had gentle, downtrodden brown eyes and a reddish mustache that contrasted oddly with his dark brown hair and was often thought to be false. His voice was so soft and gentle that he couldn't sing "Rory Get Your Dory There's a Herrin' in the Bay" without making it sound like "*Ar Hyd Y Nos*." Even for the RCMP, his record of achievement was fantastic.

Rhys took to Janet far more quickly than she to him. He had known very good women and very bad women and a great many who were neither one nor the other, though some of the variations had been interesting. This was his kind of woman. He liked the way Janet came back from the Mansion, told him it was all settled, sat him down at the kitchen table, filled his mug with tea, his saucer with pie, and his head with facts.

She talked the way she cooked, leaving out nothing that mattered and not trying to spoil the flavor with a lot of fancy touches. Half an hour later, he had a reasonably clear picture of the village, its inhabitants, and the events that had led up to his being called in. He also had another piece of pie. At last he was, for the time being, satisfied.

"Thank you, Janet. I must call you Janet, you know, and you must call me Madoc. Now I expect I'd better move my suitcase over to this house you call the Mansion before Miss Emery changes her mind."

"I told Marion you'd be eating with us, Madoc," she replied, trying out the name to get used to it. "A few days of her cooking and you'd be another case for Ben Potts."

"Ah yes, the undertaker. You haven't said much about him."

"I don't know there's much to tell. He's one of those three-monkeys types who see no evil and so forth, and his wife belongs to the Tuesday Club with Elizabeth Druffitt. The Pottses are an old Pitcherville family like the Druffitts and the Treadways and the Emerys. And the Wadmans, for that matter. I guess I told you Mrs. Druffitt was an Emery. She and Marion are first cousins. Mrs. Druffitt's father got the house, and Marion's father got most of the money and squandered it away, which is why Marion spent so much time hanging around Mrs. Treadway in the hope of another windfall. Mrs. Treadway was an Emery, too, a sister of Marion's and Elizabeth's fathers. I hope I'm not mixing you up with all this. And the Druffitts have always had a son who was a doctor, up till this generation, and the Pottses have always buried the Druffitts' mistakes for them." She attempted a laugh. "Do you suspect Ben of trying to drum up trade in a dull season?"

"It's my job to suspect everybody," he replied sadly. Even you, he thought, with your sweet voice and your cuddlesome little body and your light hand with pastry. How do I know you didn't lift that secret cache you're making such fun of, and kill the old woman and the doctor and get me up here as part of some elaborate game you haven't finished playing yet? Rhys had known even prettier women to do even stranger things.

"I suspect I'd better warn you, Madoc." Ah, now she was blushing. The rosy flush made him realize how lovely she must be when she wasn't looking so haggard. "The reason Marion's so keen on having you is that I told her you're a rich bachelor. You may be in for a pretty warm welcome."

"The warmer the better," he replied with that sad little smile. "I am in fact a bachelor, though not a very rich one. You were clever to think of such a plausible story."

"I only wish I'd been clever enough to stay out of this mess in the first place," she sighed. "Come on, I'd better walk you over and introduce you. It wouldn't look right if you went alone."

"Are you sure you feel up to it?" She did look sick. That was what made Rhys tend to believe Janet Wadman was as innocent as he wished her to be. It was always the innocent who suffered. The murderer—Rhys didn't believe in coincidences, either, especially since that second jar Olson had brought to headquarters was in fact contaminated—was no doubt happy as a clam at high water.

"I feel a little better now you're here," Janet told him. She was changing her mind about Rhys, though she wasn't yet sure why.

Marion, as expected, was waiting at the door in her new outfit, all smiles. Janet performed the introduction, and the lady of the Mansion couldn't have acknowledged it more graciously.

"Come right in, Mr. Reese. Make yourself at home."

"Thank you, Miss Emery. You're kind to take pity on a stranger."

"Listen, the pleasure's all mine. We don't get many good-looking men up here." Clearly Marion didn't intend to lose one golden moment. "You coming in, Janet?" she asked not very cordially.

"No, I've got to get back and try to straighten out that hog-pen over there. I was ashamed for Madoc to see it. You don't suppose Dot Fewter could tear herself away from the excite-ment down in the village, do you? Is your cousin's company still here?"

"They've cleared off. Trust Elizabeth not to keep the welcome mat out any longer than she has to. Gilly's with her now, writing thank-you notes."

"Where's Bobby?"

"Elmer took him fishing. So I'm here alone." She gave Rhys a meaning look.

As a Mountie, he had to be pleased that Janet took the hint and left. As a man, he couldn't help wishing she hadn't. At least getting Marion Emery to talk wasn't going to be a problem. Within minutes she was calling him by his first name and flaunting her own prospects by inviting the wealthy bachelor's opinion of Uncle Charles's self-emptying washtub.

"You're a businessman, Madoc."

He didn't say he wasn't, so she pursued the subject. "Do you think a smart old bird like Bain could be hounding us about this patent unless it's pretty hot stuff?"

Rhys scratched his red mustache. "There must be more to it than meets the eye," he ventured. There could hardly be less. Charles Treadway's patent washtub appeared as unlikely a motive for murder and arson as he'd ever come across. However, it was Madoc Rhys's mystical faith in the possibility of the improbable that accounted for his spectacular work in the field and kept him in mortal fear of being promoted to a desk job. "I'd like to meet this man Bain."

"You will if you stick around here," Marion assured her guest. "The minute he finds out we've got the patent, he'll be after us like a bloodhound. Bain's even got his son staying here to spy on us."

If the patent had been found yesterday afternoon and the old man still hadn't shown up, either Marion was exaggerating or else the son's heart was not in his work. Rhys recalled the scene Janet had described to him. Perhaps it was a genuine fight. Perhaps young Bain was righteously indignant for this Gilly Bascom's sake. Or perhaps he'd decided to play his own game.

"My cousin doesn't know about the patent, either," Marion went on. "I haven't had a chance to tell her because Henry's brothers were there. I suppose Janet told you Elizabeth just buried her husband."

"She did explain that you'd had a death in the family," he replied cautiously. "An accident, was it?"

"That's right. One of those crazy freak things. Slipped on a rug and fractured his skull on the edge of the desk. A doctor, in his own office. Can you beat that? I should think Janet would have told you all about it. She's the one who found him."

"I'm afraid Janet isn't up to talking much just now. If that hand isn't better in a day or so, I told Bert I'd run her down to the hospital." It might be a good idea to get Janet out of Pitcherville. But he wasn't here to talk about Janet. "Then this Gilly is your first cousin once removed? How is it that she's your coheiress instead of her mother, if I may be so bold as to ask?"

Marion's glance implied that Rhys might be a lot bolder than that. "Elizabeth never got along with Aunt Aggie. I never quite understood what they fought about. It was long before my time. Elizabeth is a lot older than I am, of course. I was always the favorite, actually, so it would probably all have come to me, but Aunt Aggie knew Gilly needed a helping hand. She's about as useless as an old wet sock when it comes to looking after herself. Oddly enough, Gilly's house burned down the same night Henry died. That's why I've got her living up here with me."

"You have a kind heart, Miss—er—Marion. So Gilly lost her father and her home together. Misfortunes never come singly, do they?"

"Three in a row, that's what Dot Fewter says. Dot's the so-called hired help Janet was talking about. Dot claims Gilly's fire doesn't count with Aunt Aggie and Henry because nothing got killed in it but a bowlful of goldfish. Isn't that a howl?"

Rhys obediently turned on his wistful smile. "At least Gilly must be somewhat consoled by the fact that you've found the patent."

"Gilly?" Marion snorted. "I tried to show it to her this morning before she went down to her mother's, but she just shoved it away and said, 'For heaven's sake don't bother me with that foolishness now.' Gilly's got no push at all, that's why I want to get Elizabeth in on it. You can bet Elizabeth would straighten Bain out in grand style if he tried any funny business on her."

"You wouldn't care to run down to your cousin's now?" Rhys offered shyly. "You and she could discuss your business while I see if that Dot woman will come up and give Janet a hand."

"Say, that would be swell! I'd love to have you meet Elizabeth." Marion must think her cousin would add a desirable touch of class to impress a wealthy bachelor. She was ready in seconds, but stopped short as they were going out the door. "Oops! Forgot to take this off." Quickly she untied the bright scarf with which she'd added a bright accent to her new black suit.

"But why?" Rhys murmured. "The color was so becoming to you."

"Think so?" she flashed him a smile, which was a mistake, as her teeth were not good. "I'm afraid Elizabeth might be offended if I wore it in a house of mourning. They're a lot more careful about appearances up here than we are down in the States."

They could also be a great deal more forthright. Elizabeth was perfectly capable of reminding Marion who'd paid for the outfit.

Rhys went to get his elderly Renault out of the Wadmans' driveway. He was going to be one of those eccentrics, rich enough so that he could afford to look poor. The best that could be said for his dark suit and half-soled black shoes was that they were not inappropriate for a house of mourning.

One thing Janet had forgotten to mention was that being Annabelle Wadman's cousin wasn't going to put him in favor with Elizabeth Druffitt. She received the introduction with no enthusiasm. However, she thawed noticeably after Marion managed to draw her aside and whisper something in her ear. She even called her daughter out to meet him.

Gilly was looking considerably better than she had a few days ago, although Rhys could not know that. He merely thought her a rather pleasant change from Marion and wondered if there could be brains enough behind that pale little face to plan two clever murders and a successful job of arson. She looked demure enough for any villainy in her simple black dress, with her light hair tucked back under a wide black velvet ribbon and her slim feet in ladylike medium-heeled pumps. Gilly must take after her father. There was no look of the Emerys about her, though the resemblance between Marion and Elizabeth was strong.

"I don't know how Gillian's going to manage without her dear old daddy," Mrs. Druffitt was saying. "She relied on my husband for everything after"—the well-bred voice was discreetly lowered—"her unfortunate marriage was dissolved. Poor little Gilly was only a child then, and too innocent to know—but these things are sent to test us, I suppose. My only hope now is that I may be spared long enough to see my girlie settled and happy. Gillian would make such a fine wife for the right man." This was nimble footwork for a newmade widow, but of course Mrs. Druffitt had no way of knowing how long the rich bachelor was going to be around.

Gilly gave her mother a dirty look, but all she said was, "How's Janet?"

"Not well at all," Rhys answered in a tone of gentle melancholy. "From the snapshots I'd seen, I expected a blooming young woman. It was a shock to find her looking so poorly. I understand Janet had come to consult the doctor, in fact, when—" he hesitated, as a man of delicacy might.

"Janet was here," said Mrs. Druffitt, adding a touch of frost. "I'm afraid I never did find out why. This has been such a dreadful time for me that I'm afraid I haven't been much aware of anyone's misfortune but our own. I'm sorry to hear Janet isn't well."

"In a pig's eye you are," thought the Mountie. However, he awarded her one of his fleeting, nervous smiles. "I will tell her so. I came hoping, as a matter of fact, that you could spare your—er—hired help for a day or so to give Janet a hand."

"Yes, of course, I'll be glad to, though I must say I can't promise Dot Fewter will be of much use to Janet. She certainly isn't to me. I told her I particularly wanted my upstairs bedrooms done after the guests left, but she's nowhere to be found. I daresay you might find her over at the Busy Bee. That seems to be where Dot spends most of her time."

"I've invited Madoc to stay at the Mansion till Janet's sore hand heals," Marion put in.

Mrs. Druffitt blinked. "Why, how thoughtful of you, Marion. I'm sure Gilly will do all she can to make his stay a pleasant one. Won't you, dear?"

"Sure," sighed Gilly.

After that, nobody could think of much else to say. As they were all waiting for each other to break the silence, the front doorbell rang.

"Oh dear," said Mrs. Druffitt, "would you excuse me a moment? We've had a steady stream of callers ever since—" she headed for the door, then froze. "Marion, that's Jason Bain out there."

"Jesus! Gilly, did you tell your mother we found the patent?"

"What? Of all the stupid—" Mrs. Druffitt caught herself. "Gilly, why don't you and Mr. Rhys go see if you can find Dot Fewter and take her straight up to the Wadmans'? Go along, don't stand on ceremony, please. Poor Janet shouldn't be left alone, in her sad condition."

The bell jangled yet more insistently. Mrs. Druffitt nodded a fluttered good-bye and practically shoved them out the door. Rhys caught only a glimpse of an incredibly gaunt, grotesquely spiderish figure before Mrs. Druffitt hustled Bain into the house.

"Too bad Mama gave us the bum's rush," Gilly remarked, friendly enough now that she'd got away from her guardian angel. "There ought to be one grand free-for-all when those three start grabbing for each other's throats."

"Your—er—mother's cousin did say something about a patent right," Rhys answered carefully. "She showed me the papers before we came down here."

"Did she?" Gilly replied as if she couldn't have cared less. "You can park right over there. I'll run in and see if Dot's around."

"I'll come with you." Rhys was already out of the car and holding the door for her. "I don't want to miss any of Pitcherville's historic spots."

She gave him a doubtful grin and led the way into the Busy Bee, as depressing a hovel as Rhys had ever set foot inside. The air was blue-purple with stale smoke, heavy with the reek of rancid fat. The walls were spattered with layer upon layer of grease stains. A radio blared ear-shattering noise into the murk. A blobbish creature in a filthy apron made discouraged swipes at the counter with a loathsome rag.

There was just one customer, a woman. For one incredulous second, Rhys thought it was the doctor's widow. She was sitting contentedly in the midst of the squalor, wolfing down a bright-yellow pastry with every appearance of enjoyment. When she saw Gilly, she waved.

"Hi; haul up an' set."

"No, thanks," said Gilly. "I may tend counter here once in a while, but I haven't sunk to the point where I'd hang around for the fun of it. This is Mr. Rhys, Dot Fewter. He wants you to go up to Janet's with him."

"How do you do, Miss Fewter," said Rhys politely.

"Hi," said Dot with her mouth full. "You must be the Mountie."

"The what?" Gilly gasped.

"The Mountie. Sam told me the Wadmans got a Mountie up there makin' out to be Annabelle's cousin. You're him, ain't you?"

"As a matter of fact," said Rhys unhappily, "I am."

CHAPTER 11

"Don't ast me," said Dot. "He knew, that's all. Sam always knows."

"Did he tell you why I'm here?" Rhys looked sadder even than usual as he steered the battered Renault up the hill road with Gilly beside him and the human bombshell in the back seat. Through the rear-view mirror he could see Dot shake her disheveled head.

"He ain't sure yet." He would be. Dot obviously had every confidence in Sam. "He thinks maybe it's them patents o' Jase Bain's. Jase has been spreadin' it around about how they're his o' right now that Miz Treadway's gone. Sam thinks maybe the Wadmans snuck 'em out o' the Mansion an' Jase sent you to get the goods on 'em."

"That's some fine way for that lowdown weasel to be talking about the people he works for!" cried Gilly. "If I were Bert Wadman, I'd break Sam Neddick right square in two and feed him to the pigs. I've a good mind to tell Elmer!"

There was plenty of color in that pale face now. Gilly railed on. "The Wadmans have always been a darn sight more decent to Aunt Aggie than any of her own flesh and blood, me included. The last thing they deserve is to get spied on and talked about. I expect you think you're pretty smart, Mr. Rhys or whatever your name is, worming your way in there, making believe you're Annabelle's long-lost cousin just because she's flat on her back in the hospital and can't show you up for a liar. Well, let me tell you one thing—"

She had to pause for breath, and Rhys got his word in. "I'm here at Janet Wadman's request."

"But—but why?" Gilly stammered.

"I'm sorry, but I'd really prefer not to answer that question just now. And I'd greatly appreciate it if you could manage not to tell anybody else who I am. Miss Fewter, have you repeated what this Sam Neddick told you?"

"Only to my mother."

Gilly snorted. The Mountie sighed. "Is there any hope of your persuading her to keep the secret?"

"Are you kiddin'? Ma must of told at least seventeen people already." Dot sounded rather proud of her mother's prowess as a newscaster.

And those seventeen had told seventeen more and by now he was being discussed over every back fence in Pitcherville, no doubt. The best-laid plans of mice and Mounties went oft agley.

"Then, ladies, may I ask you one great favor?"

"What's that?" said Gilly suspiciously.

"Could you pretend that you still think I'm Annabelle Dupree's cousin, and let things go on as they have been?"

"You mean let you go on staying at the Mansion, and call you Mr. Rhys, and all that?"

"If you please. Madoc Rhys happens to be my real name, by the way."

"And you don't want us to tell Marion, or even Elmer?"

"Not even Elmer. Believe me, it's for your own sakes as well as mine that I'm asking."

"What do you mean by that?"

"I'm afraid I can't answer any more questions just now."

Rhys wasn't really trying to be enigmatic; he simply needed time to think. He did not care to explain the situation to Gilly Bascom here and now, and he'd much prefer not to tell Dot Fewter anything, ever. No doubt she'd find out fast enough anyway.

He only wished he knew how this Sam had found out who he was, and why the hired man had been so quick to broadcast the information. Was Sam trying to get a warning to somebody he didn't dare approach in person? Was the message intended for Rhys himself, a tactful way of letting him know he had a fat chance of getting anywhere in Pitcherville?

Had the leak come inadvertently from Fred Olson or from Janet herself? Did Neddick have The Sight? There was a lot of Highlander blood in the Maritimes. Rhys felt an eldritch stirring under his own skin. It was a bad sign when a case started going sour like this right at the start.

Gilly Bascom had, after all, been properly brought up. Realizing Rhys meant what he said about not explaining, she did the right thing and changed the subject. "My mother's sore at you, Dot. She was expecting you back to clean the bedrooms after Uncle Clarence and Uncle Edgar left."

"Oh rats, I clean forgot! An' that reminds me I left my satchel with my overnight things in it at her house. I'll have to go back an' get it. Maybe I can give Janet a hand gettin' dinner an' then ast Sam to drive me back down. I could run a mop around for your mother an' then come back to the Wadmans' for supper."

Dot appeared delighted at the prospect of all this backing and forthing. Not knowing that her jubilation was mainly due to the prospect of getting to eat at the Wadmans' twice in one day, Rhys deduced that she was anticipating the joy of spreading fresh gossip between the hill and the village. She was her mother's daughter, no doubt of that. Though probably, he thought with venom, not her father's.

He dropped both his passengers at the Mansion and went over to the Wadmans' alone. At least he could break the bad news before Dot Fewter beat him to the draw. He found Janet sitting out in the porch swing with a book, looking somewhat less beaten.

"How did you make out with Marion?" she asked. "I saw the pair of you go off together."

"Marion was no problem. As for the rest, it's a bust. Where's your brother?"

"Down at the barn milking, I should think. Why, what's wrong?"

"I was hoping I might get to him before your hired man

does. This Sam chap has told Dot Fewter that I'm a plain-clothes policeman, and Dot has told her mother. Have you any idea how he got his information?"

He was watching the tired, fine-boned face as he spoke, but saw only anger and resignation.

"It's my fault," said Janet bitterly. "I should have warned you about Sam. Don't ask me how he did it, but I might have known he would. He just picks things out of the air."

The haunted look was back. Rhys felt an urge to take her capable little hand and pat it, but discipline is strong in the Force. He gave her a few kind but noncommittal words instead, and headed for the barn. Bert was there, not milking yet but raking straw and manure out of the stalls. He kept his cows as clean as his sister did the kitchen. A decent, thrifty, hard-working lot, the Wadmans.

"Hi, Cousin Madoc. Come to see how a farmer earns his living?"

"I don't have to be shown, thanks. I've raked enough muck in my time. You can drop the cousin bit, Bert."

"Huh?"

"Then your man Sam hasn't got around to telling you yet? Not to beat around the bush, I'm a detective inspector from the RCMP."

Bert held the identification card at arm's length, squinting to read it because his eyeglasses were back at the house. When he handed it back, all he said was, "Does Janet know?"

"Janet's the reason I'm here." As neatly as if he were filing a report, Rhys explained. Bert shook his head in disbelief.

"Why the hell didn't she tell me?"

"She figured you'd be safer not knowing."

"Safer? My God, nobody's after us, are they?"

"Since you ask me, I'd say it's entirely possible. Have you any idea where I might find this Sam of yours?"

"Hell, he's not mine. Sam's his own man if anybody ever was. You might try the upper pasture. I've been after him to reset some fenceposts there." He pointed out the way, and Rhys followed it.

Rhys didn't really suppose it mattered whether he found Neddick or not. Rhys had run across this sort before, humans with a beast's awareness but not always an animal's innate sense of decency. More like wolverines than anything else. He'd learn exactly as much from the hired man as Neddick wanted him to know, and he'd have that information carried to him somehow whether they ever met face-to-face or not.

Sam Neddick was an unlikely suspect in this case, anyway. If he'd wanted Mrs. Treadway dead, she'd simply have died and there'd be no loose ends left hanging for a clever woman like Janet Wadman to catch hold of and wonder about. Henry Druffitt's death might be more Sam's style, but a handyman ought to know enough to make the right kind of wound.

On the face of it, this looked to be one of those dumb-luck jobs a scared rabbit like Gilly or a clumsy opportunist like Marion might pull off and maybe succeed in, but he knew better than to form any theory yet. He still had too many unknown factors to resolve, such as Charles Treadway's patent washtub.

He wished Elizabeth Druffitt hadn't been so expert about getting rid of him as soon as Jason Bain showed up. It had been a superb demonstration of what a ruthless, quick-thinking woman could do, though. He could see Elizabeth killing for money except that she apparently didn't stand to get any and wouldn't have needed it. Her own parents' bequest and her thrifty ways ought to keep her eating even though the doctor had turned out so inept at bringing home the bacon.

With her penchant for family feuds, her tightfistedness, and her domineering ways, Elizabeth Druffitt should in fact make a likelier victim than a murderer. Was somebody trying to get at her by first eliminating the aunt and the husband? It would seem an oddly roundabout approach.

As Rhys had more or less expected, the upper pasture was empty, although a row of raw fenceposts showed that Sam had been there not long before. A whiskey-jack was giving the job a critical inspection. Rhys watched the Canada jay for a few minutes, then wandered back to the gray hulk of the Mansion. He found Gilly Bascom alone in the house, making beds.

"Here, let me do that." Rhys twitched a quilt over the sheets as deftly as any housewife. "There's a lot of work to a place this size."

"And darned little help, I can tell you. Thanks, Madoc." Gilly pushed a lock of two-toned hair back under her headband. She was still wearing the black velvet ribbon though she'd changed the black dress for a print coverall that would better have suited an older and taller woman.

"Will you be staying on here?" he asked for the sake of starting conversation.

"I don't know. My mother wants me to. The place I lived before wasn't grand enough to suit her." Gilly tossed a pillow on the bed and slapped it viciously into place. "Mama'd be willing to let me slave eighteen hours a day so she could bring those old biddies up here to tea once a year and show them what sort of style her daughter lives in."

There didn't seem to be any tactful reply Rhys could make to that, so he said nothing. They made up the rest of the beds together, then he ran the dry mop around the painted floorboards while she dusted. At last Gilly remarked, "Well, at least we've got these rooms looking halfway decent. I never could manage that in my little dump, no matter how hard I tried."

"Still you were sorry to see it go?"

"In a way, yes. It was only a shack and the Lord knows it didn't hold many happy memories, but that house was mine. Not like this place, which is supposed to be half mine but will always be Aunt Aggie's as far as I'm concerned. Without my own place, I'm—floating. I felt more adrift watching that fire than I did when my husband walked out on me. Though neither of them was anything much to anchor onto," she added with less rancor in her voice than might have been expected.

"If it weren't for Elmer being here—" She flushed, and began rubbing the dustcloth violently over one of her great-aunt's mahogany side tables. Then she dropped the duster and leaned toward him, her thin fingers smudging the top she'd been working so hard to polish. "Madoc, is that why you're here? Is it about my house?"

He nodded. "Partly, yes." Why was she looking so terrified? "Gilly, you know that fire was set, don't you?"

"I was always so careful," she whispered.

"Do you know who set it?"

"No! No, I don't. Honest, Madoc."

"Do you know how it was set?"

She shook her head. "I don't know anything. But I'd left Bobby asleep by himself, and I know I couldn't have—" Gilly Bascom was not the difficult sort of hysteric. She merely dropped into one of the green plush chairs and huddled there in an agony of silent suffering. Rhys was in the bathroom fetching her a tumbler of water when an enormous man and a skinny boy burst into the house and up the stairs.

"Ma! Hey, Ma, where are you?" the boy was yelling. He had a fishing pole in his hand and almost took the Mountie's eye out with the end of it as he raced past without noticing that a strange man was in the house. "Ma, look what I caught! Mama, what's the matter?"

"Gilly, what's the matter?" echoed the young giant who must be Elmer Bain.

"N-nothing. I was remembering about the poor g-goldfish. We'll get some more, honey."

Gilly was blowing her nose on the duster, trying to laugh at her own breakdown. A good mother in spite of the hair. The child was showing her his catch of trout, not very big ones but creditable enough for a beginner.

"Elmer taught me how to clean 'em, even. I did it all by myself. Mostly, anyhow."

"Thank goodness for that! Elmer, you were great to take him. Come on, let's show Janet and ask her how to cook them. I'd hate to spoil such beautiful trout. Boy, won't they taste good!"

Either expecting Rhys would tag along or more likely forgetting all about him, Gilly led the others across the side yard toward the Wadmans'. The Mountie gazed after them somewhat wistfully for a moment, then shrugged and got back to work. He might never get another chance like this for an unchaperoned tour of the Mansion.

Here was the library where Janet had discovered those papers Bain wanted, stuck in a book with a giveaway title. How could Marion Emery have missed so pointed a clue if she'd searched as thoroughly as she claimed to have done?

Here was the kitchen where Agatha Treadway had died, and here were the cellar stairs. He went down. The basement was surprisingly bright and clean-looking for a house of this vintage. He'd have expected a floor of fieldstone or trodden dirt, but this was a whitish composition he'd never seen before. He soon realized how it had stayed so fresh-looking: The surface was flaking off on his bootsoles. Another of the late inventor's brainstorms, no doubt. Looking at the leprous blotches he'd collected, Rhys wondered more than ever why Jason Bain should lust after one of Charles Treadway's patents.

And here were the rows of shelves where Mrs. Treadway had kept her home-canned provender. Had he been inclined to doubt Janet Wadman's tale of the mismatched string beans, he'd have waived disbelief now. His own mother was no slouch with a preserving kettle, but Agatha Treadway had been an expert of experts. Every jar was meticulously filled, its wire bail clamped firmly over its grooved glass lid. Every little red tongue of every rubber sealer ring stuck out bright and pert. Janet had told him Mrs. Treadway would never have been foolish enough to use the same ring twice, and clearly she hadn't.

He found the thirteen jars of string beans, each one with its contents unmistakably snapped in contrast to the poisonous pint that Fred Olson had so thankfully turned over to his colleagues. They'd got hold of the lab report on the pint that had killed Mrs. Treadway. The finding of botulism had been clear, but there was no statement as to whether the vegetables had been cut or broken. By now, of course, that first specimen would have been discarded and whoever did the analysis wouldn't be able to remember. Even should the technician care to venture an opinion, which wasn't likely, it probably wouldn't count for much as evidence.

If Dr. Druffitt had lived, there'd be another story. A jury would have listened to him. He'd been at the scene, he'd collected the evidence. Mrs. Treadway had been his patient and his wife's aunt. He'd have had sound reason to recall every detail about that deadly jar. Rhys would have one clear-cut case of murder to work on, instead of two probables and no proof.

He might be able to get an exhumation order on Henry Druffitt, though the family would surely fight him on account of the scandal, but what was the use? There was the medical certificate all in order. Dr. Brown was still reasonably compos mentis, for what that was worth. Olson said Mrs. Druffitt was home by the time Dr. Brown arrived to make his examination, and from what Rhys had heard of that courtly old gentleman, he'd be the last to notice anything that might distress a lady.

As to that dent in Henry Druffitt's skull, Rhys didn't doubt that it had in fact been the wrong shape when Janet and Fred Olson felt it, but it was surely the right shape when he was buried. Either the obliging Ben Potts or the enigmatic temporary assistant Neddick would have made sure of that.

CHAPTER 12

Rhys hung around till Gilly and her menfolk came back and gave him a halfhearted invitation to join the fishfry, then he politely declined. He had other fish to fry. A Mountie's lot is sometimes not a happy one. He had no intention of denying himself such fringe benefits as came his way, such as a chance to look at Janet Wadman while he ate.

Like any good housewife, Janet was profuse in her apologies as she set a feast before him. "I'm sorry it's such slim pickings around here tonight. I just can't seem to think straight, much less cook right. Dot Fewter never did come back. She's going to stay down with Mrs. Druffitt tonight. I suppose the poor woman's afraid to sleep in the house alone. At least Dot's better than nobody."

"That's a matter of opinion," said Rhys. "This food is delicious, Janet, and I shall help you with the dishes. Where's your brother? Doesn't he want to eat with me?"

"He was too excited to eat with anybody. Mama Dupree—that's his wife's mother—called up and said they'd just told Annabelle she could leave the hospital, so he hared right on down there without even stopping to wash his hands, much less eat his supper. It doesn't matter, Mama Dupree will give him something. She sets a beautiful table."

"No better than yours, I'm sure," said Rhys with all sincerity. "Then Bert will be bringing his wife here tonight?"

"Oh no. Annabelle's going to stop on with her folks for a week or so. She wouldn't be able to stand the ride up here yet, and she still has to see the doctor a couple more times at the hospital. I expect Bert will sleep over with them and drive back about daybreak. That's what he usually does."

"Then who will do the chores tomorrow morning?"

"Sam Neddick, I expect, if Bert's not back in time. Sam lives right next door, you know, in the loft over Mrs. Treadway's barn. I guess I told you that before. I do feel awful about that business with Sam. I should have warned you. We're so used to him, I just didn't think."

"Please don't blame yourself, Janet. I only wish I knew how he does it."

"He's a snoop, for one thing. Can't you manage another spoonful, Cousin Madoc? I don't know why I keep calling you that."

"I've been called worse." Rhys passed his plate without further coaxing. "What are the chances of getting anything out of Sam, do you think?"

"Slim, unless there's something he wants you to know."

"You don't surprise me. But Janet, if your brother's going to be away all night and Dot isn't coming, that means you'll be here alone, unless—" Her Majesty the Queen might not care to have him pursue that line of thought much further. Anyway, Janet didn't seem worried.

"I've stayed alone at least two nights a week for the past month. One more won't kill me, will it?"

He sincerely hoped not. "You're sure this was a bona fide call?"

"What? Oh, you mean—" Janet laughed uncertainly. "No, we've known for the past few days the doctor was planning to release her any time. I took the call myself, and it was Mama Dupree on the line all right, and the kids were all excited, I could hear them asking when Daddy was coming, and Grandpop Dupree was right there telling her what to say and she was shushing him the way she always does. That sort of bedlam would take a lot of faking. Besides, when I went to tell Bert, he came straight in and phoned Annabelle at the hospital to make sure, because Mama Dupree does get things twisted sometimes. She needs a hearing aid and won't admit it. And Annabelle said yes and to come as quick as he could because she couldn't stand being away from him and the kids one more minute than she had to. I don't know why I'm going on like this."

Rhys gave her one of his shy smiles. "It's natural enough. Would there be any more tea in the pot?"

"I guess likely." She smiled back, a good deal more attractively. "What were you planning to do after supper?"

"What would you suggest?"

"I don't know anything about detecting."

"Sometimes I wonder if I do. Suppose for the sake of argument that I really were a visiting cousin. What would be the program then?"

"Sit around and chin about the relatives, I suppose. Or I could show you over the farm or maybe take a walk down by the pond. It's pretty there when the fireflies come out, provided the mosquitoes don't join them."

"There's a little breeze tonight that should help to keep the bugs down. I vote for the pond. Where is it?"

"Straight down at the end of the road, only the road doesn't go that far."

"How far goes the road go?"

"Depends on what sort of mood Bert's in when he's out with the mower. Officially it stops just past our house."

"Then nobody lives beyond you?"

"No. There's never been any family on the hill except the Treadways and the Wadmans that I know of."

"Then who owns all the land around here?"

"We do. Marion and Gilly will get everything from the Mansion down to the town road, and the rest is ours, pretty much. Bert's and Annabelle's, anyway. I've been meaning to sign my share over to them ever since I was twenty-one, but they keep talking me out of it. They'd like to see me come back here and settle some day, which is natural enough, I suppose. There aren't many of us Wadmans left, and now Annabelle won't be able to have any more."

She looked sad about that. Rhys changed the subject by asking, "And when were you twenty-one?"

"Last October. I'm getting to be an old woman."

"That makes you about seven years younger than me, so I must be a very old man."

They laughed together. Seven years was a comfortable enough span between a man and a woman. Rhys wrenched his mind back to real estate.

"Then Gilly's and Marion's inheritance is a sizable one. There's considerable acreage in that parcel."

"Yes, but the land's not worth much," said Janet. "We got the best of it. Theirs is mostly ledge. That's why the Mansion is built so close to the property line. It was the only place they could dig deep enough for a foundation. Anywhere else you'd hit rock within a foot or two. You can't build on it, can't farm it, couldn't even graze anything except maybe sheep or goats."

"Has anyone ever tried?"

"A contractor came over from Moncton a few years back, pestering Mrs. Treadway to sell him a strip down by the road. Now that we have the highway, Pitcherville's not quite so far off the beaten path, and a lot of people who have buildable land are figuring to make their fortunes in a few more years. Mrs. Treadway would have sold, but after the man had done a little exploratory digging he backed off."

"And nobody else has come forward?"

"I shouldn't suppose another builder would care to get stung any more than the first one did. Madoc, are you sure you've had enough to eat?"

"Janet, I could not be surer. Why don't you go rest yourself in the rocking chair while I give you a demonstration of how we supersleuths wash dishes?"

"Don't be silly. You can dry if you want."

"I'll wash and you dry, so you won't get your bandage wet."

"All right. Then I can wipe off what you miss."

"I never miss. We Mounties always get our grease spots."

"Just don't get them on your suit. Here, let me give you an apron."

His chosen profession had led him into many vicissitudes. Rhys supposed he could handle a ruffled lavender-checked apron. Janet was amused, and who was more entitled to a spot of innocent merriment than this dear, brave young woman who had been through so much? Than this dear, brave young woman who'd been next door when Mrs. Treadway succumbed to botulism and in the next room when Dr. Druffitt got his skull bashed in? Rhys reminded himself that Janet was as likely to be guilty as anybody else, but he wasn't listening to himself and knew he wasn't. He wore the apron and washed the dishes and found the experience pleasant.

When they'd finished the task and got the kitchen tidy, Rhys untied the apron and handed it back to Janet. "Now what shall it be, relatives or fireflies?"

"I expect you'd like the walk."

"If you feel up to it."

"Oh, I think I could stagger that far. Maybe the fresh air will do me good."

The sun was modestly gathering a few clouds around itself before taking the evening plunge. They strolled down the path from the house, not saying much. Over by the Mansion, Elmer and Bobby were having a game of catch. For a while they could hear shouts and laughter and the yapping of whichever dachshund wasn't upstairs nursing her pups. Then they couldn't hear much except wood thrushes singing their version of "The Bell Song," and some crows having a political argument.

The path got rougher as it began to descend. Rhys, being a loyal officer of the Queen, found it his bounden duty to give the weak and afflicted a helping hand. The weak and afflicted accepted his aid with a smile that showed a dimple he hadn't realized she possessed. Decidedly, Janet Wadman needed a great deal more investigating. He wondered if she'd care for a rendition of "Rose Marie." Not being Nelson Eddy, he wisely abstained, but retained possession of the afflicted's hand as Her Majesty would naturally expect him to.

The pond, he found, was worth coming to see. It had all the requisite panoply of peaceful waters, overhanging leafy branches, exquisite water lilies clustered about picturesque snags of fallen forest giants, and even the fringe benefit of a green heron fishing in the shallows on the opposite shore. They watched the tall bird catch his supper, flip the small fish expertly down his throat, then flap off to digest his meal at leisure in some cool roost.

"You have a nobler nature than I, Janet," said Rhys at last. "I don't think I could ever sign away my share of a spot like this."

"Neither could I," Janet admitted. "Perhaps it's well we don't own it. Our land stops back there on the ridge."

"Then who owns the pond?"

"It's still part of the Treadway estate, far as I know. The Treadways were Loyalists who came up here from Boston at the time of the American Revolution. New Brunswick was formed as a Loyalist colony, as you doubtless know. Anyway, they got a big land grant at that time. Bert could probably tell you how many acres. They sold some of it off to the lumber companies over the years, and our farm to my great-grandfather when he came out here from England, but they kept title to this little strip around the pond. Great-grandfather didn't need it, you see, because we have that other little pond out by the lower pasture for the cows to drink from, and I guess nobody else ever wanted it. The pond's not good for much, except to look at."

"Don't you ever come here to swim?"

"Oh yes, though you have to be on the lookout for snapping turtles. Some of those old snappers could nip your toes off. But the water's lovely, though it never warms up much. It's fed by underground springs, you see. Oh look, there's the first lightning bug. And," she slapped at her bare arm, "the first mosquito."

Rhys didn't want to leave, but duty compelled him to suggest, "Shall we start back before we get eaten alive?"

The "we" was pure gallantry. The mosquitoes were ignoring him in favor of Janet's more succulent epidermis, as what sensible bug wouldn't?

They climbed back to the ridge where the breeze was

brisker and the mosquitoes fewer. It was impossible not to pause and look back. Dusk was deepening now, and the fireflies were putting on some impressive pyrotechnics.

"Such a beautiful, beautiful place," Janet sighed. "I used to dream about it down in Saint John. I wish our folks had bought the pond years ago. I hate to think what might happen to it now."

"What could happen?" said Rhys, knowing full well.

"Lots of things, I'm afraid. We never gave it a thought as long as Mrs. Treadway was alive because we knew she'd never do anything to hurt us, but once Marion gets a clear title, she'll sell it to anybody who comes along. Some rich so-called sportsman, like as not, who'll cut down all the trees to build him a fancy lodge and fly in parties by helicopter. They'll be staggering out blind drunk to take potshots at anything that moves, polluting the pond, scaring off the herons—"

"And the snapping turtles," Rhys added gravely.

"Well, the turtles were there first, weren't they?"

"Couldn't you get in your offer first?"

"We could if we had the money, I suppose. Marion will want top dollar, you can bet your boots on that. As it is, I suppose Bert will just have to put up a fence and pray."

"Of course, if the place became popular, Bert himself could sell out to a developer for a tidy sum."

Janet gasped, as though Rhys had said a particularly dirty word. "Bert would never sell! This farm is his life's blood. He'd die if he ever had to move."

Rhys nodded. He'd known of people who'd died from having to leave their home acres. He'd known of others who'd died of trying to hang onto them. The case was taking on new ramifications, and he was liking it less and less.

CHAPTER 13

Rhys bade Janet a chaste good night, went back to the Mansion, and settled into his assigned bedroom. When Marion, Gilly, and the rest were safely bedded down for the night, he sneaked out, went back to the Wadmans', and kept vigil on the porch hammock. He encountered no marauders except two raccoons, a family of formally attired skunks, and a number of wild rabbits. As dawn began to show gray over the cowsheds, he crept back to his lodgings and got into bed.

Because there was nothing special to get up for, he allowed himself to sleep till nine. He'd told Janet not to expect him for breakfast since he could always get something at the Mansion and didn't know what he'd be doing after that. She'd said not to be too sure about breakfast and the teapot would be on the stove if he got desperate. A beautiful woman.

He could see that Bert's car was back, so things must be under control over there. There was some secondhand coffee in the percolator and a box of sugar-coated frosty pops or some such abomination laid out on the kitchen table with a bowl and a spoon thoughtfully placed beside it. He ignored them, brewed a pot of strong tea, and cut a thick slice from a loaf that Janet must have contributed. After this simple but satisfying repast, he wandered into the yard.

Elmer, Gilly, and young Bobby were out in the new dog run, throwing sticks and laughing as the dachshunds beetled after them. Rhys wanted to talk to Gilly, but hesitated to go over, knowing his presence would put a damper on their fun, and her bodyguard would inhibit a free exchange of conversation. He desired a word with Marion, too, but she didn't appear to be around.

Rhys sauntered out front and on down the hill road, noting that the property around the Mansion was indeed extensive though rocky and sparse-looking, and that it afforded a fine view of the valley across from the excellent new road that ran down into the village. Both the would-be developer and Pitcherville's expectant tradesmen must have been disappointed when this appealing site proved unfit for building.

There wasn't another house for almost a mile; then he began to encounter dwellings, decently kept up for the most part, each with its patch of bright annuals in front and its well-tended plot of pole beans and cabbages and turnips and whatnot around at the side. Pitcherville was a self-respecting place.

It was too hot to be walking with his coat on, but he kept his shirt sleeves buttoned and his sober tie knotted under his loosened collar. It wouldn't do to make himself too comfortable since he was, after all, on duty. Behind every clean pair of parlor curtains, at least one pair of eyes must be watching every step he took, and by now they must all know who he was. How many of these respectable folk had reasons of their own to wonder why he was taking such an interest in their houses?

Rhys had no trouble finding Fred Olson's garage, or its proprietor. Olson was sitting on a broken-down kitchen chair in the doorway, chewing on the stem of an unlighted pipe.

"Good morning, Marshal."

"Mornin', Inspector." Olson got up and dragged out a second chair. "How's it goin'?"

"I haven't the faintest idea," Rhys told him. "I'm just stirring around to see what floats to the top. I expect you've heard the Mounties are in town."

"Yep."

"Have you any idea how Sam Neddick spotted me?"

A grin flickered momentarily around the pipestem. "Says you pinched 'im once in Moose Jaw for disorderly conduct."

That could have meant almost anything, and probably had. Rhys smiled back ruefully. "Old pinches have long memories."

"Sam never forgets nothin'."

"Or forgives, obviously. I shan't get any help from him."

"Not likely."

They sat for a while without talking. Olson exchanged his unlit pipe for a surprisingly dapper gold-banded briar, stuffed tobacco into the bowl, and puffed until he all but disappeared in smoke. At last his voice came out of the cloud. "They're claimin' Jase Bain called you in to get 'is patent back from Elizabeth Druffitt. I don't know who started that one. Ma Fewter, like as not."

"But why Mrs. Druffitt? It was my understanding her daughter inherits from Mrs. Treadway's estate, not she. Can't Gilly Bascom handle her own affairs?"

"Huh!" The marshal rapped out sparks on his boot heel and stuck the fancy pipe back in his shirt pocket. "Rhys, tell me the God's honest truth: Do you think there's anything to that patent business?"

"Do you?"

"Hell, no! Everybody's been bustin' their britches over Charles Treadway's foolish inventions since before I can remember. I'm too old to start believin' in fairy stories. Only if that patent ain't worth nothin', then what was the sense of anybody killin' Miz Treadway?"

"How valuable would it have to be?"

"How'm I s'posed to answer that one? Ten dollars could be a lot o' money if a person was flat busted."

"Do you know anybody who's that hard up?"

"I don't imagine Gilly Bascom's got two nickels to rub together right now, but Gilly's always had 'er folks behind 'er, and now there's the inheritance to borrow against if she needs to. See, that's how it goes in a little place like this. Everybody's got somebody, as you might say. Most of us never have any ready money to speak of, but we're in no great danger o' starvin' to death. We know there's always a handout to be got somewheres."

Olson hesitated. "O' course I'm speakin' for Pitcherville. I wouldn't know about foreigners."

"You're referring to Marion Emery?"

"Well, I did get as far as algebra though you mightn't think so, an' I'd say she's what our teacher used to call the unknown quantity. Her father was a brother of Elizabeth's, but as they say, there's good eggs an' bad comes out o' the same basket. I was only a little-bitty kid when Phil Emery pulled out for the States but I know he was never welcome back. Too many girls' fathers after 'im with shotguns. I dunno if he married Marion's mother or not. I s'pose his luck was bound to run out sooner or later, though, so he must of. Anyways, she started comin' up here seven or eight years ago faithful every few weeks to see dear old Aunt Aggie. 'Twasn't as if Miz Treadway wanted 'er. Accordin' to Dot Fewter, not that you can put much stock in anythin' she says, ol' Aggie treated Marion like dirt under 'er feet. Hell's bells, would you sit up all Friday night on a bus an' then turn around an' do the same thing Sunday if you wasn't mighty anxious to get your meathooks into some ready cash?"

"But Marion's been working regularly down in Boston, hasn't she?"

"So she claims. I dunno what at, but it can't o' been much if she was willin' to throw up 'er job just like that soon as Aggie died."

"She no doubt expected a larger inheritance," said Rhys. "Didn't you say it's going to work out at about five thousand dollars apiece for her and Gilly?"

"Five thousand in cash plus a half interest in the property an' whatever might or might not come out o' that patent Jasé Bain's so set on gettin' hold of. Don't seem like much, but you never know." He reached for the fancy pipe again. "I s'pose it might look just as good to Gilly Bascom, maybe better. Gilly's done some awful foolish things in 'er time. But, damn it, Inspector, I can't see any woman burnin' down her own house with herself an' her kid an' them two little dogs inside. Can you?"

"Not easily."

Rhys thought of the young mother back at the Mansion sitting on that uncomfortable Victorian chair, sobbing her heart out. It was never safe, as he knew from sad experience, to exonerate a woman because she cried. She might have been feeling guilty because the fire had got going faster than she'd thought it would and the risk had been greater than she'd anticipated. She might have been having an attack of nerves. Or she might have started crying to keep him from asking too many awkward questions.

Faking an attack on yourself was the oldest trick in the murderer's book. What good was it to have money behind you if you also had a tightfisted mother holding the purse strings and refusing to loosen up unless you made impossible concessions? And what if you were in love with a chap your mother didn't approve of, and what if that chap had been brought up to respect the value of a dollar and wasn't about to take unto himself a somewhat shopworn bride without some cash on the barrelhead? Rhys stood up and dusted pipe ashes off his pantlegs.

"Well, I expect I ought to get on with the job."

"Where you goin' now?"

"I thought I might as well mosey over and explain to Mrs. Druffitt that she's had a couple of murders in the family." The woman had to know sometime, if she didn't already. Rhys had no doubt that the grief-stricken widow would be able to withstand the shock of being told.

Janet had explained to him that the Druffitt house was in fact the Emery house. The widow still lived in the dwelling where she was born, while the doctor's ancestral home had been cut up into a lawyer's office, presumably the one so well patronized by Jason Bain, a couple of stores, and the Owls' Hall. They could both have used a fresh coat of paint. Rhys noted this not very interesting fact as he went up the steps and rang what had been the doctor's bell.

Dot Fewter answered his ring, greeted him in an oddly subdued manner, and went to tell Mrs. Druffitt that he'd arrived. She then came back and lurked in the shadows, pretending to dust. Rhys was not surprised when Marion Emery accompanied her cousin into the foyer, or that both women met him with cold and sour looks. Even had they known Rhys was in fact a bachelor with a modest inheritance from a great-aunt of his own prudently salted away in the bank, they probably would have been no more cordial. Vipers in the bosom were clearly not their cup of tea.

"Well, Mr. Rhys," said the doctor's widow, "it appears we have been made the victims of a deception."

He returned her Medusa glare with an apologetic smile that barely twitched the corners of his mustache. "I only wish the deception could have been maintained a while longer, Mrs. Druffitt."

"I didn't tell 'em," the hired help broke in. "They already knew when—"

"That will do, Dot," snapped the mistress of the house. "Go back upstairs and finish your dusting."

She motioned the other two into her late husband's office and shut the door behind them. Rhys noted that the jamb was edged with felt weatherstripping and judged that the room must be almost soundproof. The murder might well have been accomplished without Janet's hearing while she sat in the waiting room just outside.

Elizabeth Druffitt took the doctor's chair behind the desk. Marion Emery sat down in the one no doubt intended for the patient. Rhys was left standing, like a poor relation about to be refused a loan.

"I daresay you ladies are wondering why I came."

It was a feeble enough beginning. Marion snorted. Her cousin's long upper lip curled. These expressions of scorn did not put Rhys off. He was used to them.

"The reason is," he went on in his gently plaintive voice, "that the Mounted Police have been called in to investigate the murders of Agatha Treadway and Henry Druffitt."

Both women went gray as the smoke from Fred Olson's pipe. "I don't believe you," Marion gasped. "What is this, another trick?"

Rhys shook his head. "No, it is not."

"But that's crazy! Auntie died of food poisoning. I was

there. I—" she caught her breath, her skin now the color of old putty. "Are you trying to pin something on me?"

"Shut up, Marion." The doctor's widow was gripping a handsome polished onyx pen stand, her knuckles shiny yellow knobs against the black stone. "Explain yourself, Mr. Rhys."

"As you know," he said, "Mrs. Agatha Treadway died of botulism, having eaten improperly preserved string beans. We have evidence that those particular vegetables were prepared by someone other than herself with malice aforethought, and that she was tricked into eating them."

Neither of the cousins made any reply to that. They simply stared at him, their long, gaunt faces astonishingly alike. After a long time, Mrs. Druffitt said quietly, "And my husband?"

"Your husband died as the result of a skull fracture."

"I know that. He slipped on that little braided mat right over there, and hit his head on the edge of this desk."

"No, he did not, Mrs. Druffitt. He was struck from behind with a heavy, rounded object, similar to the head of that brass poker out in your waiting room. His body was then arranged in such a way as to make the death appear accidental."

"Do you expect me to believe that?"

"Frankly, Mrs. Druffitt, our investigation will proceed whether you believe it or not. You will find the result easier to accept if you do, of course."

Marion opened and shut her mouth once or twice, but the look on her cousin's face silenced her. At last the doctor's widow spoke again. "Do you have any evidence?"

"Oh yes, plenty of evidence. We don't go around making up wicked stories to frighten innocent people with, you know."

"Then," the woman let go of the pen stand and ran her long fingers carefully across her forehead, "I suppose I must believe you, mustn't I? This—this is a terrible shock. You must give me time—"

"Certainly, Mrs. Druffitt. I understand how you must feel."

Actually, Rhys was not at all sure he did. Marion Emery's reaction was easier to interpret. She was eyeing him with the trapped look of the born underdog. That didn't necessarily mean anything. Guilty or innocent, she must realize she was bound to rank high on his list of suspects.

• "Now, ladies," he went on in a fatherly tone even though both were a good deal older than he, "I'm sure you realize it will be in your own best interests to work closely with me in clearing things up as quickly as we can."

"But the talk! What will people think when you start going around asking all sorts of dreadful questions? Think of the gossip!" For the first time, Mrs. Druffitt's agitation sounded wholly genuine.

"I had thought of that," Rhys answered. "That was why I tried to pass myself off as a relative of the Wadmans. I was hoping to conduct my investigation so unobtrusively that no-body would realize anything was being investigated." He smiled sadly. "Unfortunately, I ran into an old acquaintance."

"I should call it more tragic than unfortunate." The widow was pulling herself together now, sitting up taller in the cracked-leather swivel chair, the bones in her face standing out like an anatomical diagram. "Our position in this community—"

Marion said something nasty. Her cousin glared.

"Marion, I'll thank you to remember that you're in my house."

"Knock it off, Elizabeth. If you think it's any distinction to be an Emery, go take a look at that slut who's probably got her ear glued to the keyhole right now. You know damn well why they kicked my old man out of Pitcherville, and you also know he didn't get the habit from anybody strange. I'll bet there's hardly a soul in this village who isn't related to us one way or the other, mostly the other."

If looks could have killed, Rhys would have had another corpse on his hands as of that moment. However, Elizabeth Druffitt only said, "That will do, Marion. I'm sure Mr. Rhys doesn't care to hear any more of your gutter talk, and neither do I." She turned to the inspector with a gesture of apology.

"I'm grateful that you appear to see the difficulty of my situation, even if those who should know better choose to treat it as a subject for levity. I shall certainly help you in every way I can. The sooner this terrible scandal is hushed up and forgotten, the better for all of us."

Hushing up scandals was hardly part of his job, but he deemed it impolitic to say so at a time when co-operation was being offered. "Thank you, Mrs. Druffitt. That is very sensible. Now, since you are willing to help me, perhaps you and Miss Emery wouldn't mind answering a great many questions."

He took the two women with agonizing thoroughness through the recent events and a great deal more. He went into family history, village history, details of Charles Treadway's wildly checkered career as an inventor, anything he could think of that would keep them talking and possibly turn up a word or two of useful information.

Once they saw the relatively impersonal trend his interrogation was taking, they stopped being cagey and showed themselves eager to answer in detail. After two hours in that hermetically sealed office, his head was splitting from the sounds of their voices. It was a relief when he at last got around to Jason Bain's interest in Uncle Charles's patent washtub. All of a sudden, the ladies didn't care to talk any more.

CHAPTER 14

Rhys trudged back up the hill, his mind full of questions and his shoes full of gravel. His stomach, on the other hand, was distressingly empty. Mrs. Druffitt hadn't offered him so much as a cup of tea and he'd decided that eating at the Busy Bee called for valor over and beyond the call of duty. Though it was now long past the noon hour, Janet would give him something, bless her kind heart in advance.

That long conversation with Marion and her cousin had given him nothing, so far as he could determine, except a shrewd hunch that they had made or were about to make a deal of some sort with Jason Bain about the patent. He would learn nothing more about that from any of them. His best hope was that Dot Fewter really did listen at keyholes. She'd be up later, she'd told him, to help Janet with the supper. He could wait.

In fact, he waited with deep contentment. Janet, having heard his tale of gastric woe, poured him a slug of Bert's rum to soothe his nerves while she prepared a snack of ham and eggs, brown bread and strawberry jam, fresh tomatoes from the garden, fresh lettuce from the patch by the back door, and a modest wedge of apple pie with cheese to stay his stomach till suppertime. After that, he adjourned to the glider hammock on the porch to collect his thoughts, and fell asleep. When he woke, Dot Fewter had arrived.

Dot was, as he had confidently expected, eager to tell all and then some. Her prize nugget of intelligence was that Jason Bain had called on the widow again shortly after Rhys had left, stayed half an hour or so, and gone away looking like the cat that had swallowed the canary. She deeply regretted that despite her most determined effort she had not been able to overhear a word of the interview. Dr. Druffitt's office was indeed well soundproofed.

What had happened after that? Marion had gone out to do some shopping. She'd telephoned to the Mansion before leaving, asking Elmer to meet her at the market in half an hour, and Dot had it on reliable authority that Elmer had, in fact, done so. As to what Marion had bought Dot couldn't say, but no doubt she'd be able to before the day was over.

Rhys was not interested in Marion's grocery list. "And how did Mrs. Druffitt seem after the others had left? Was she pleased with the result of Bain's visit? Upset?"

"She don't generally show her feelin's much unless I happen to break somethin'," Dot answered reflectively, "only today she was—I dunno how you'd call it. Kind o' sad an' thoughtful. She was real nice to me, too."

"Was that so unusual?"

"I'll say it was! I dunno, I guess she'd got to feelin' low in her mind about the doctor. She went pawin' through his desk an' found the picture they took of 'im the time he got to be Grand Supreme Regent at the Owls, an' brought it out into the parlor an' stuck it up on the pianna. 'I think I'll buy a silver frame for it,' she says to me, so I says to her, 'They're awful expensive, ain't they?' an' she says to me, 'Money isn't everything, Dot,' an' I tell you that give me a queer feelin' right down to the pit of my stomach. An' then you'd never guess what she did!"

"Probably not," said Rhys. "Would you care to tell me?"

"Well, I'll be darned if she didn't take me upstairs an' open her closet door an' take out that lilac dress she was wearin' to the Tuesday Club meetin' when Dr. Druffitt brained hisself. 'Here, Dot,' she says, 'somebody might as well get the good out of this. I'll never wear it again.' She gimme the whole outfit: hat, bag, shoes, white gloves, everythin'. O' course they ain't new but they're beautiful quality. I never thought I'd live to see the day! Ma was flabbergasted when I told 'er."

"Then Mrs. Druffitt was not in the habit of passing such things on to you?"

"She never passed nothin' to nobody, never before in 'er life, far's I know. You could o' knocked me over with a feather! O' course she couldn't o' worn 'em again for a year anyhow, 'cause she'll be in mournin'. Most folks don't bother no more, but Mrs. Druffitt likes to do things proper."

Yes, that had been Rhys's impression. Propriety was, he would have said, the essence of Mrs. Druffitt's character, so why did she choose to accentuate the likeness which Marion had so ungently pointed out to her not long before, by dressing a woman who was no doubt her illegitimate cousin in her own distinctive castoffs?

Perhaps she wasn't thinking about such things any more. Could it be that she'd had a sudden onrush of Christian charity and decided it was time to let bygones be bygones? Was it simply that she couldn't bear having the clothes in the house any more because of their association with her husband's murder, and that she gave them to the maid because that was what ladies were supposed to do with their hand-me-downs? He must ask Janet's opinion when he got her alone.

However, he didn't get her alone. Bert came bouncing in to supper, rejoicing at Annabelle's release from the hospital and the prospect of having his family reunited under their own roof. Dot was much in evidence, wolfing down everything that came her way. Rhys resented her presence, not only because she ate like a whole messhall full of starving loggers but also because she'd be there to help with the dishes instead of him. He would have rejoiced in another such session as last night's. Wearing the lavender apron would be a small enough price to pay for the chance to stroll down by the pond and watch the sun set behind the soft brown cloud of Janet Wadman's hair. But it was not to be, and anyway duty lay elsewhere. Humming a mournful snatch of *"Gogoniant i Gymru anwylwlad fy nhadau,"* he crossed the side yard to the Mansion.

Marion, to his deep regret, was there alone. "I'm baby-sitting," she explained. "Elmer took Gilly to the movies to get her mind off Henry and I'm stuck here with the kid. Isn't it just my lousy luck you turned out to be a cop instead of a rich bachelor from Winnipeg? Oh well, maybe I'm due for a break. It's about time, God knows."

Marion's attitude was an interesting mixture of apprehension and smugness. She was plainly nervous with Rhys, but he also got the distinct impression she thought she was putting something over on him. In any event, though she was cautious, she was not overtly hostile. "What the heck, as long as we're stuck with each other, we might as well make the best of it," was her cordial remark as she fetched the cribbage board and a deck of cards.

They played a couple of rounds amicably enough, then Marion got up again and came back with two juice glasses and a dusty-looking bottle. "Want to try Uncle Charles's most successful invention? Elmer found a hidden cache while he and Janet were looking for the patent. The old gink made the best cherry brandy in the world, and never got around to writing down the recipe."

She poured them each a glassful of the dark red liquid. A sip warned Rhys that the stuff was as lethal as it was delicious, and he nursed his drink henceforth with due respect. Marion either didn't realize or didn't care. She downed the stuff like barley water. By half-past nine her shrewd game had gone to pieces. By a quarter of ten she could barely find her pegs, let alone count the holes on the board. As the mantel clock struck ten, Rhys dragged her inert form to the couch and threw an afghan over her.

He went back to the cards, played a few hands of Canfield, finished his first and only glass of cherry brandy because it would be flying in the face of Providence to waste any, and went upstairs. Gilly and Elmer were still out. Bobby was safe asleep with one of the dachshunds on the bed beside him, its long nose stretched out on the pillow and a stubby paw resting against the boy's shoulder. Rhys went to his own room and put on his pajamas.

The cherry brandy turned out to be a powerful soporific. Rhys might have slept on like the lotus eaters had he not been violently aroused. The time was 6 A.M. and the rouser was Marion. She was slapping him, shaking him, screaming into his ear. "Madoc, for God's sake, wake up! She's dead!"

"Who?" He sat bolt upright regardless of his canary-yellow pajamas.

"Elizabeth," she moaned. "Out there on the lawn."

He was out of bed, grabbing for his trousers, barking at her to go wake Elmer. He'd got his coat on over his pajama top and was tying his shoelaces so he wouldn't break his neck running down the stairs when she screamed, "They're gone!"

"Who's gone?" he yelled back as he bolted for the staircase.

"Gilly and Elmer. Their beds haven't even been slept in. And Bobby's gone, too!" she shrieked over the bannisters.

She was still yelling something when he rushed out the door. It took less than a second to spot the woman's body sprawled on the sun-brown grass, a bundle of lavender and white print, and a tumble of black hair.

"That—" Marion was at his elbow. "Madoc, is that—?"

"Keep back. Don't come any nearer."

Rhys himself picked his way toward the body, watching where he put his feet, but the hard-baked ground told him nothing. He knelt and carefully pushed aside the blood-matted hair. The face exposed looked like Elizabeth Druffitt's, but was not.

"It's Dot!" Marion screamed. "It's Dot Fewter wearing Elizabeth's dress. What's she got Elizabeth's dress on for?"

"Marion, be quiet." Rhys didn't need hysterics on top of everything else. "Dot was telling us last night at suppertime that your cousin had given her some clothes. However, she was not wearing this dress then. She had on some sort of loose—er—garb with broad red and green stripes."

"That's right." Marion was trying to calm herself, although her voice was shaking. "She had that tent shift thing on yesterday morning when she came to clean down there. Elizabeth blasted her out for wearing such a getup to a house of mourning and made her put on an old gray cotton housedress of Elizabeth's own. But Elizabeth didn't give it to her, she only lent it. Elizabeth never gives anybody anything."

"The outfit in question was the one your cousin had been wearing when her husband was murdered, and she gave it because she said she could never wear it again. Does it seem unreasonable to you that a woman should wish to be rid of clothes that had such unhappy associations?"

"I don't know. I guess not."

"Would this be the dress your cousin wore that day?"

"Maybe. I don't know. She'd changed to black by the time I got down there."

"But this is in fact one of her dresses?"

"Of course it is. God knows I've seen it enough times, that and those damned genteel Cuban-heeled pumps with the little bows on the toes, white in summer and black in winter. Elizabeth never wears anything else; that way she can get by with only two pairs. It looked so strange yesterday with the temperature up to eighty and her wearing black shoes. Look, Dot's even got the shoes on. Madoc, is she really dead?"

"You seemed sure enough when you were hauling me out of bed," he answered rather testily. "Why are you asking me now?"

"I—I don't know." Marion licked her lips. "Look, what are you driving at? I didn't touch her, if that's what you mean. I never went near her. I just got up to go to the bathroom and looked out the window and—and here she was out here on the ground and—and Elizabeth would never—"

Rhys nodded. It was true. From what he could judge of her, Elizabeth never would. And the woman before him was indeed dead, no doubt of that. Had been for at least four or five hours if he was any sort of judge, which experience entitled him to be. He explored the mess of hair with his fingers, hating the feel of it, and found a deep cavity on the crown. It was rounded, like the one Janet Wadman and Fred Olson claimed to have felt in Dr. Druffitt's fractured skull.

Had the same weapon been used? Then why wasn't the wound cleaner? Why were crumbs of fresh earth sticking to the blood clots? He looked around and saw whitewashed rocks the size of cabbages outlining the driveway. One of them was a trifle out of line. A few sprigs of yellowed grass showed where it had been replaced, neatly but not quite neatly enough.

CHAPTER 15

So it was that simple. The killer had simply grabbed the first heavy object that came to hand, and whanged away. He'd then carefully put the rock back where it belonged, but left the corpse lying where it fell. Why? It would have made more sense to drag Dot over to the border and lay her head against the rock, as though she'd tripped in those unaccustomed shoes and fallen.

It would have been a bit difficult to place her properly, though, since the injury was in such a curious place, on the top of her head and slightly to the front, as though somebody had stood face-to-face with her, lifted the rock high above her head, and brought it down with all force. But why should she stand there like a fool and let herself be struck down?

Maybe she hadn't been standing. Maybe she had in fact tripped and was sitting on the ground when it happened. Maybe the killer had come pretending to help her up, bent over her, and hit her instead. That would be easy enough even for a small person. In any event, the nature of the injury suggested it had been done by somebody she knew and wasn't afraid of. That didn't help much. Dot would have known just about anybody from around these parts. She'd been too long on good nature and too short on brains to be easily frightened.

There was something finical about the way that rock had been replaced. The act suggested a housewife with tidy habits and too little strength to move a tall, big-boned body like Dot's. Somebody like Gilly Bascom, who liked to leave a place looking halfway decent, as she'd remarked while they were making the beds together. Somebody—and Rhys did not enjoy this idea—like Janet Wadman with her injured hand.

There was also the boy Bobby. Could he, with the fantastical reasoning of a child, have imagined he could clear himself of suspicion by putting back the weapon?

But why should any of these three, or anybody at all, want to kill Dot Fewter? Maybe nobody had. Here was a woman the size of Elizabeth Druffitt, wearing a distinctive and familiar outfit of Elizabeth Druffitt's; a light-colored outfit, moreover, that would be easy enough to recognize in the dark.

It was not unreasonable that Elizabeth might have decided to break her long boycott of the Mansion and decide to spend a night here with her daughter and her cousin, rather than sleep alone in her own place. It was not unreasonable that she might find herself unable to sleep at all, and try to calm her nerves by a late-night stroll around the yard. Mightn't somebody else have made the same mistake Marion did when she saw the body on the lawn?

Marion could even have made that same mistake twice. She'd have needed great powers of recovery, though, if she'd been able to stagger out here and commit a murder so soon after she'd passed out over the cribbage board. On the other hand, she might have been a good deal less drunk than she'd appeared to be. It was possible that his own faculty of discernment had been a trifle impaired by the time he dragged her to the couch.

Rhys was rather taken with that hypothesis. For one thing, it took Janet Wadman and her brother off the list of suspects. They'd known about the dress. Marion and the rest of them at the Mansion had not, so they could all be left on. So could the rest of the town, for that matter, unless Dot had managed somehow to get the word around in the brief time she'd had between leaving Mrs. Druffitt and coming to Janet. It appeared to be an accepted fact of life around here that Elizabeth Druffitt had never given away any of her possessions and never would.

Mrs. Druffitt made a far more logical victim than Dot Fewter. Mrs. Druffitt had a husband who'd just been murdered, so she constituted a possible threat to whoever had done that little job. She had property, she had power and influence in the community. Under that ladylike façade she had the gall of an ox. She also, he was willing to bet his Sunday boots, had by now worked out a deal of some sort with Jason Bain. That combination of circumstances suggested several possible motives.

Rhys slid a couple of twigs under the rock and lifted it gingerly on to a sheet of paper he'd asked Marion to bring him from the house. It was a letterhead captioned "Treadway Enterprises Ltd," he noticed. He wasn't concerned with letterheads; he was thinking about the chance of fingerprints on that whitewashed surface. A vain hope, no doubt. Anybody who'd take the trouble to put back the rock would be tidy enough or clever enough to wipe it off, most likely. Even young boys. Especially young boys. They read comic books, and watched cops-and-robbers programs on television.

Elmer, Gilly, and Bobby were all three missing and presumably all three together. The two grownups, if such they could be called, must have got back from their movie sometime after Rhys and Marion had been lulled to rest by Uncle Charles's lotus-blossom brandy, picked up the child, and cleared out. What better reason could they have for doing so than the one that lay here in front of him?

They couldn't have known Rhys would be asleep, unless they'd fixed it up with Marion beforehand to dose him with the brandy. That would mean they'd planned the crime in advance. But they wouldn't have expected Elizabeth Druffitt to be here, so Dot would then have to be the right victim, after all. And what would Dot be doing here when she was supposed to be over with Janet?

He tried another tack. Suppose for the sake of argument that Bobby had skinned out of the house after Rhys had found him so sweetly asleep with his canine bedmate. Suppose the boy had got up to some mischief or other, not necessarily anything really wicked but something he wouldn't want to get caught at, and been appalled to run into a woman he thought was his grandmother as he was sneaking back into the Mansion?

According to Janet, Bobby had been in trouble before. Mrs. Druffitt, being the sort of woman she was, would certainly have taken it upon herself to censure him for his misdeeds. With the terror of the fire coming directly on top of his grandfather's death, who could tell what state of nerves he might be in? Might he not have panicked, grabbed up a rock from the border, and—what? Stood on tiptoe and asked his grandmother to bend over so he could bash her skull in?

What would any boy do with a rock? He'd throw it. He might not mean to hit, only to divert the woman's attention long enough for him to get away without being caught. But that rock would be a heavy projectile for a boy his size, and his aim could have gone amiss. Gilly and Elmer could have come home to find a terrified youngster crouched on the lawn beside a blood-stained corpse. Their natural, though certainly not overbright, reaction might very well have been to hustle the boy into the car and take off.

Rhys went into the house, called RCMP headquarters, and asked for a road watch to be got out for a 1976 green Ford sedan presumed to be carrying its owner, Elmer Bain of Pitcherville, along with a short, slim blonde woman and a boy about ten years old. He had no great confidence they'd be picked up. Elmer might have sense enough to ditch the car. If they got off into the woods and young Bain was any sort of woodsman, they might elude capture for a long time. The weather was warm, there was plenty to eat in the forest if a person knew what to look for, there were fish in the streams and rabbits for the trapping. They could work their way west or north or south, perhaps down over the border. Elmer probably had some money on him. They might even split up, take different buses or trains, and meet in Toronto or somewhere a good way from here.

Well, wherever they were, he was here and there was work to be done. He took up the phone again and called Fred Olson. "Fred, you and your friend Sam Potts might as well

come up to the Mansion. Tell him he's got another customer."

"Lord God A'mighty," cried the marshal. "Who is it this
time? Janet Wadman?"

"No!" Rhys managed not to add an unprofessional expression of gratitude. "It's Dot Fewter."

"You hauled in Sam Neddick yet?"

"No, I have not."

"How come?"

"Because I'm a fool," the Welshman replied sadly. "Make
it quick, will you, Olson? I need somebody to take charge
here while I go after Neddick. Oh, and stop at the Druffitt
house on your way. See if Gilly Bascom and her son are there,
with or without Elmer Bain. They've all three turned up
missing."

Olson said, "Right," and hung up. A good man. Pitcherville was luckier than it knew.

"They won't be at Elizabeth's." That was Marion, tagging
close to Rhys as if afraid to be alone, for which he couldn't
blame her, considering her resemblance to the dead woman
out in the yard.

"No, I don't expect they are," he replied, "but we have to
check, you know. You have no idea where they might have
gone?"

Marion shook her head. "None whatever. All I know is
they tried to kill me and then took off."

"Tried to kill you? Marion, do you really believe that?"

"Why the hell shouldn't I? If Gilly gets rid of me, she inherits Aunt Aggie's whole estate, doesn't she? And why
should anybody want to kill Dot Fewter, unless it was a mistake? Look at her. She was my size and build, had features
like mine, hair like mine. She was here in my yard where she
had no business to be at that hour. Okay, she was wearing
Elizabeth's dress, but why shouldn't Elizabeth have passed
that outfit on to me instead of Dot? I was down there yesterday, too, wasn't I? I'm Elizabeth's own legitimate cousin instead of her God-knows-what. I'd have got a lot more wear

out of it than that Fewter bitch, wouldn't I? My God, what am I saying? I ought to be damned glad she didn't!"

Rhys scratched his mustache. "Did you talk with Gilly at all before she and Elmer went out last evening?"

"Sure. We had supper together. That's when she asked me if I'd mind staying with Bobby because Elmer'd offered to take her to a show. I said yes, because what the hell? I wasn't doing anything else anyway."

"Did you repeat to her what I told you and her mother yesterday?"

"About Henry and Aunt Aggie being murdered? Yes, I did. Why shouldn't I? It's as much her worry as mine."

"Of course it is and there is no reason why you should not have told. How did she take the news?"

"How does she take anything? Sat there staring at me like a scared rabbit."

"Did she make any comment?"

"Just swallowed a couple of times and said, 'Thanks for telling me, Marion.' I don't know what to think." Marion shook her head as if it ached, which it probably did. "I was beginning to like Gilly."

"One must not jump to conclusions," Rhys reminded her gently. "Perhaps you can go on liking her. Was Elmer present when you gave Gilly this information?"

"No. I waited till he and Bobby went out to feed the dogs. Speaking of which, I guess I'd better go do it now before they start yapping their fool heads off. I cannot for the life of me see Gilly going off and leaving those little puppies like this. I'd have thought that was the last thing she'd ever do."

"Do you think it possible Elmer may have taken her against her will?"

"Listen, buster, where that guy's concerned, she hasn't any will."

"Listen, buster," was hardly a respectful form of address to a member of the RCMP, but Rhys had long ago accepted the fact that it was no good trying to stand on his dignity. He merely inquired, "You don't recall seeing or hearing any sort of commotion during the night?"

Marion grinned sheepishly. "After I passed out, you mean? You should know better than to ask. That stuff's dynamite. Didn't it get you, too?"

"I slept soundly," Rhys admitted. "Marion, tell me the truth: Is that why you gave it to me? Did Gilly suggest that you try to get me plastered?"

She gaped at him in honest surprise. "Hell no, I just figured it would liven up the party a little. I was feeling lower than a floorwalker's arches, if you want to know, finding out about Aunt Aggie being murdered and figuring I was probably first in line for the hot squat. And then Gilly going off on a date with a good-looking guy while I—oh hell! It's my birthday next week and I'm going to be forty-seven, if you want to know."

"Being forty-seven is perhaps better than not being forty-seven," Rhys reminded her gently.

"Yeah, I guess you can say that again." Marion darted a frightened glance out the window. "What a rotten break for poor old Dot!"

"She may not have been killed in mistake for you, you know," said the Mountie. "It's more likely that she was mistaken for your cousin Elizabeth. It is also quite possible that she was killed by somebody who knew perfectly well whom he was killing. Where would I be apt to find Sam Neddick, do you think?"

Marion brightened visibly. "My God, I never thought of Sam! I guess I'm not wrapped too tight this morning. There's no telling where he'd be by now if he did this. If he didn't, I suppose he's over milking Bert Wadman's cows, unless he overslept. You might look up in the hayloft. That's where he lives, when he lives anywhere. Aunt Aggie let him use it in return for doing her chores. What's the matter? You look funny."

"So I have often been told," said Rhys. "Would you mind

getting something to cover Dot with? I'd as soon not try to move her until Olson gets here."

Marion went and got the crocheted afghan she herself had been bundled up in the night before. "Will this do?"

"Fine," he replied.

She tagged after him when he went outside, as if she couldn't bear to stay alone. Since she was going to hang around anyway, Rhys decided she might as well make herself useful. "Marion, I'm going inside the barn to see if Sam Neddick's there. You stay out here and watch for Olson, will you? If anybody else comes, or if you find you can't endure being here, don't come after me but simply call. I promise I shan't go beyond shouting distance."

"Okay."

She gave him a doubtful attempt at a grin, and he went.

CHAPTER 16

The hired man's aerie was surprisingly elegant. It contained an ornate brass bedstead with a mangy blue-velvet cover and a marble-topped commode that held a flowered ironstone pitcher and washbowl, neither of them too badly chipped. There was also a cheap but flashy modern dresser on which stood several bottles of men's toiletries—gifts, no doubt, from the demised girlfriend. Sam wouldn't be apt to use them himself, unless he got really thirsty.

Neddick wasn't around. Marion's analysis was doubtless correct. He must either be hard at work or over the hills and far away. There were plenty of signs that he'd entertained Dot Fewter often enough in his exotic boudoir: long black hairs on the velvet counterpane, a filthy powder puff thrown down among the colognes and after-shave lotions, a hopelessly laddered pair of pantyhose under the bed. It was a safe enough bet that she'd either been on her way here or going back from the barn to the Wadmans' when she was attacked in the drive. A romantic tryst would account for her having bothered to put on the hand-me-down finery.

Rhys didn't stay in the loft more than a minute or two. Marion was still over by the body and didn't appear to be in too bad a state, so he called out, "Neddick isn't at home. Do you mind if I go over to the Wadmans'?"

She flapped her hand, in either protest or permission. He took it for permission, and went. Sam was the first person he ran into. It had to be Sam, because the man looked exactly as Rhys had pictured him, of no particular age with a face and neck the color and texture of old boot leather and a perfectly blank expression. His body was neither tall nor short, a bit humped at the shoulders but no doubt strong and quick as a lynx when speed was necessary. The eyes were almost without color, like two miniature crystal balls.

"Been lookin' for me?" he grunted.

"Expecting me to be?" Rhys grunted back.

"Yep."

"Then why didn't you come and find me yourself?"

Sam just leaned on the manure fork and looked at the Mountie with those crystal-ball eyes.

"Was she on her way to visit you when she was killed, or had she already been to the loft?"

"She'd been."

"What time did she leave?"

"Midnight, more or less."

"Did you walk out to the door with her?"

"Hell no, I stayed in bed. Must o' been asleep before she was out o' the barn." There was a twinge of regret in the bereft lover's tone. Was Neddick sorry his sweetheart had been murdered, or sorry he'd missed the chance to watch it happen?

"You realize," said Rhys with all the sternness he could manage, "that you're in serious trouble, Neddick?"

Neddick spat over the manure fork.

"How do you propose to get yourself out of it?"

"Figgered I'd leave that to you, Inspector."

"Did you, now? Can you give me one good reason why I shouldn't take you in this minute?"

"'Cause you'll look like a jeezledy fool when you have to let me go," Neddick replied calmly. "Hell's flames, Inspector, you know damn well if I'd o' wanted to get rid o' the poor cow, I could think o' seventeen better ways than lammin' her over the head an' dumpin' the corpse in my own dooryard."

He spat again, not quite so forcefully. "But why would I want to? Answer me that. She was handy an' willin', an' she didn't cost me nothin' but a dollar's worth o' jellybeans or somethin' now an' then. An' she was sort of a likable bitch when you got to know 'er. To tell you the truth," Neddick confessed in an embarrassed mumble, "I'm goin' to miss 'er."

Rhys gazed into the crystal balls for a while, and divined that the man was probably telling the truth, or a reasonable facsimile thereof. "Can you think of anybody who might have had it in for her?"

Neddick jabbed the tines of his pitchfork into the ground a few times, then slowly shook his head. "No, can't say as I do. Don't make no sense to me at all. Dot had an awful big mouth, but there wa'n't no more harm to 'er than a kitten."

"Might she have found out something that somebody didn't care to have told?"

Amusement flickered for an instant over the leathern face. "She gen'rally did. Only she'd always blat it out to the first person that come along. I'd o' known, for sure."

"But suppose this was something she didn't know she knew?" Rhys persisted.

"Come again?"

"I mean some apparent trifle she wouldn't think worth repeating."

Sam thought this was pretty funny, too. "There wa'n't one jeezledy thing on the face o' this green earth Dot wouldn't think was worth repeatin'. Cripes, if Hank Druffitt lost a button off his union suit at seven o'clock in the mornin', every last, livin' soul in Pitcherville would know it by eight."

"Why? Was Dot playing around with the doctor?"

"Hell, no. She done their laundry. Dot never fooled around with nobody. She knew I wouldn't stand fer it."

"Then what would you say to the possibility that your friend was murdered by mistake?"

"I'd say that was one hell of a big mistake." Neddick scratched a shoe-leather ear. "Maybe that's not such a dern fool notion as it sounds, Inspector. That gownd she had on, eh? Any time that bitch give anythin' away, she might o' known there was no luck in it. Made 'er look the spittin' image of 'er, an' I told 'er so point-blank."

"Do you mean it made Dot look like Mrs. Druffitt, or like Marion Emery?"

Neddick actually looked surprised. "Now you mention it, I guess it could o' been either. Them three was like as peas in a pod, which ain't surprisin', all things considered. I hadn't thought o' Marion, but she'd make more sense, wouldn't she, if you're talkin' about a mistake. Hell, she was right there in the house an' it stood to reason the bitch might o' give her them clothes instead o' Dot. I wisht to God she had!"

"Why? Would you like to see Miss Emery out of the way?"

"Hell no. I got nothin' in partic'lar against 'er. Not yet, anyways. Only one I can think of might like to get rid o' Marion would be Gilly Bascom, 'cause then she'd get the Mansion all to 'erself. 'Cept Gilly's got it in for 'er mother a lot worse'n she has for anybody else. An' if that was 'Lizabeth Druffitt layin' out there," Neddick spat again with force and vigor, "I'd be proud to shake the hand that done it. An' I ain't goin' to say no more than that."

"If you choose not to, I shan't try to force you," said Rhys mildly. "I wonder if you'd do yourself and me one favor, though, Neddick. I'd just like to have you walk back over there with me and take a close look at Dot Fewter. I'm curious to know if there has been any change either in the way she was dressed when she left the barn or in the way she was lying when you saw her earlier this morning."

Sam didn't say he would but he didn't say he wouldn't so Rhys started back and as he expected, the other man fell into step with him. Marion was still on sentry duty beside the afghan-covered object on the grass, but she shrank back into the doorway when they got near her. Either she was afraid of Neddick or else she wanted Rhys to think she was.

Rhys folded back the afghan, careful not to disturb the folds of the dress any more than he had to, and waited. Neddick gazed down at his deceased lady-love, the crystal eyes blank as hers. At last he made utterance.

"She put 'er shoes on."

"Explain that, please."

Neddick pointed contemptuously at the dainty pumps.

"She didn't have 'em on when she left. She'd carried 'em over in 'er hand from the Wadmans' to show me, as if I give a damn, but she was in 'er bare feet 'cause she didn't want to get 'em dirty. She'd just cleaned 'em, see?"

She certainly had. Rhys had never before observed a pair of shoes so lavishly whitened. Dot had managed to slather polish all over the tops, the heels, and under the insteps, getting a good many daubs on the soles in the process. The left shoe was half off, and he could even see dribbles of white on the lining. Evidently the poor soul had been determined to do full justice to her distinguished hand-me-downs.

"She can't have walked far in them," he remarked.

"Prob'ly couldn't if she was o' mind to," Sam grunted. "I don't see why she bothered to put 'em on at all. They must o' been awful tight. See the way that right foot's swole out over the top? She was always bitchin' about 'er feet hurtin' from bein' on 'em so much. Miz Treadway used to say by rights she ought to complain about 'er backside instead 'cause she was on that a damn sight oftener. Ol' Aggie had a tongue on 'er, I can tell you! Cripes, both of 'em gone an' me standin' here like this."

He shook his head, as if to clear it of unmanly sentiment. "Nope, that's all I can see, 'cept that somebody's pushed the hair back from 'er face. I s'pose that was you? I never touched 'er, myself. Didn't have to. I knew, just lookin' at 'er." Neddick bent and with something like tenderness pulled the afghan back over the body. Then he turned back toward the Wadmans' barn.

Rhys got neatly in his way. "Neddick, what do you know about that patent Jason Bain has been creating such a rumpus about?"

"Not a jeezledy thing."

"Come, now, I think you can do a little better than that. Would you say he has a legitimate claim to the thing?"

"It's possible," Sam admitted. "Jase likes to do things legal if he can."

"Have you the vaguest idea what he expects to get out of it?"

"No, I ain't, an' that's a funny thing." The colorless eyes narrowed. "Jase has been talkin' awful free about the bundle he's goin' to make out o' that patent. Usually when he's up to some deal you can't get a yip out of 'im, 'less he's suin' somebody. Then he's got it all spelled out in dollars an' cents 'cause it's a matter o' record anyways. But this is a new one on me. Here comes Olson."

Rhys could hear nothing, but he had every confidence that Sam was right, and Sam was. Seconds later, Pitcherville's one excuse for a police car hove into view and stopped at the drive.

The marshal was still working his paunch out from under the steering wheel when the other door swung open and Elizabeth Druffitt erupted. "Where is she?"

"Right here, Mrs. Druffitt." With deliberate cruelty, Rhys uncovered the body again.

Mrs. Druffitt gave the corpse one almost totally uninterested glance, then grabbed his arm and began shaking it. "I mean my daughter. Where is she? What has he done with her? Answer me!"

"I wish I could, Mrs. Druffitt," said Rhys. "All I can say is that the police are doing everything they can to track her down."

"The police? What good are they? You're a policeman and you let her go off with—with that!" Suddenly Mrs. Druffitt appeared to realize that she had a dead woman at her feet. She gave the body her full attention for a moment, then turned on Rhys with a fresh tirade.

"There, you see! Can't you understand what he did? That's my dress she has on. He thought he was murdering me! And you've let my daughter—my only child—"

Now she was totally hysterical. Among them, the two men and the cousin managed to get the distraught woman into the Mansion.

"Marion, look after her, will you?" begged Rhys. "Make her a cup of tea or something."

"Tea!" moaned Mrs. Druffitt. "He can talk about tea!"

"Come on, Elizabeth, you'd better go lie down." Marion got an arm around her cousin and steered her into the library. Rhys had hardly begun giving Olson a rundown of what he knew thus far when she was back in the kitchen.

"Elizabeth fell asleep practically the minute she hit the couch. Do you think she's all right?"

● Rhys went in and took a look at the unconscious woman. Her breathing was regular, her pulse seemed normal. "Shock does that sometimes," he told Marion. "I also shouldn't wonder if your cousin took a sedative last night and is getting a reaction from it now. In any event, sleep is far the best thing for her under the circumstances. Get a blanket and cover her up, then leave her alone for a while."

He went back to Olson. "Marshal, I'm going to leave you in charge here for a while, if you don't mind. Have you notified Potts?"

"Yep. He'll be along as soon as he gets his pants on."

"Good. I have a camera in my car and I'll take a few pictures of the body as it lies right now. When he comes, have him take it down to his place but tell him not to do anything more until we can get somebody up here for an autopsy. I'll arrange that. Two in a row might be a bit much for your Dr. Brown. And keep your eye on this saucepan."

Rhys showed Olson the paper-wrapped rock, which he had packed into one of Mrs. Treadway's cooking pots for want of a more convenient receptacle. "As far as I know, this was the murder weapon. I'm going to have it checked for fingerprints, so don't let anybody touch it unless he wishes to be counted as a suspect."

Marion came back and asked, "What shall I do now?"

"Be ready to assist the marshal in any way he wishes, and answer the phone if it rings. Write down any messages for me, and please be sure you get them exactly as given. If your cousin should wake up and become hysterical again, you might try some of your uncle's cherry brandy on her."

She answered Rhys's smile with an equally melancholy one of her own. "I think I'll take a few slugs myself."

"A pot of strong coffee would do you more good. No doubt the marshal could use some, too. I have to go now."

Janet should be up by this time, getting breakfast for the men when they came in from the milking, probably wondering what Fred Olson's car was doing over here at the Mansion and fuming a bit because Dot Fewter hadn't come downstairs to help her. She'd wonder why he was coming to get the camera from his car and then going back to the Mansion with it. It was obviously his duty to go in and explain what the commotion was all about. If she happened to invite him to stay for breakfast, it would be cruel and insensitive of him not to accept. Duty must indeed be done.

CHAPTER 17

"I can't get over it! Only last night she was sitting right here at the table, happy as a—" Janet's lovely, sensitive mouth began to quiver and she tried to steady herself. "Well, at least she died on a full stomach, poor soul. Couldn't you eat one more of those doughnuts, Madoc?"

"Thank you, Janet, but I could not. Do you recall exactly when you last saw Dot?"

"Let me think. Bert went to bed right after supper. He was worn out from all the excitement over getting Annabelle back to her folks'. Then Dot and I watched some foolish program on TV that she was crazy about, don't ask me why. So it must have been just after ten when we went upstairs. She called me into her room to show me an outfit Mrs. Druffitt had given her."

"Did you recognize the clothing?"

"How could I not? Mrs. Druffitt had it on the day her husband was killed. I suppose that's why she didn't want it around any more, though I must say if they'd been mine, I shouldn't have cared for the notion of letting Dot Fewter go parading in my things down to the Busy Bee or up to the haymow with Sam Neddick."

"If you'd been in her place, you'd have given them, say, to Marion Emery?"

"Why yes, I suppose I would. Marion's her own cousin, after all. The only one she admits to, anyway. Besides, Marion will be going back to Boston sooner or later, I expect, so she could wear the clothes down there, where nobody would know where they came from. I'll bet Marion's—" Janet caught herself, and shuddered. "No, I expect she's just as well pleased. Not pleased, I mean, but—"

"I know what you mean," said Rhys, fighting an impulse to offer comfort in a more emphatic form. "I think you could safely say that she is at least somewhat relieved. Tell me: How did Dot seem to you last evening? Would you say she was at all worried or preoccupied about anything?"

"Heavens no! She was tickled silly. She'd had a good supper and enjoyed her program, and she was so proud of that new outfit—" Janet choked a little.

"Did she say anything about showing it to Sam Neddick?" said Rhys quickly.

"No, though I might have known they had a little something cooked up between them. To tell you the truth, it never entered my mind. That was the one thing Dot never talked about and of course Sam didn't, either, though everybody's known for years what was going on."

"Then anybody who knew she was staying with you might have guessed where she'd wind up before the night was over?"

"I should think so if they'd had their wits about them, which I obviously didn't."

"However, it's not likely anybody would expect her to be wearing Mrs. Druffitt's clothes?"

"I'd doubt that very much. Dot hadn't had time to show them around the village, and it's not like Mrs. Druffitt to give anything away as a rule, not even to the church rummage sales. Dot used to complain that Mrs. Druffitt wouldn't even give her a cup of tea without measuring out the milk and sugar as if it were gold."

"Would you say that just about anybody from around here would have recognized Mrs. Druffitt by her clothing even if her face was not visible?"

"Oh yes, no question about that. She wears the same things year in and year out, and she takes a pretty dim view if anybody tries to 'copy her style,' as she puts it. Though why anybody would want to is beyond me. Madoc, you don't think somebody killed Dot thinking she was Mrs. Druffitt?"

"Would that idea make sense to you?"

"Yes, I suppose it would," Janet replied slowly. "Or even if they thought it was Marion. Anybody but poor, silly Dot Fewter. Oh Madoc, I just don't think I can stand any more!"

She was wearing a sleeveless pink wraparound. Since it was part of the Mounties' code to handle witnesses with utmost tact, Rhys decided he might tactfully administer a comforting pat to her smooth, warm shoulder and steady her hand while she drank a calming tumbler of water.

"I'm afraid you think I've muffed this case pretty badly," he remarked in mournful tone.

"Oh no!" She looked up at him, her large hazel eyes starred by lashes stuck together with tears. "How could you have prevented this? How were you to know Dot would make a beeline for the barn as soon as the rest of us were asleep? How could you know she'd be wearing Mrs. Druffitt's clothes? How could you know somebody was waiting out there to hit her over the head with a rock?"

She began sobbing again. Rhys, the very soul of tact, continued to massage her pleasant shoulder blade. At last she reached for a paper serviette from the holder on the table, and blew her nose.

"Madoc, may I ask you a question?"

"Of course."

"This has nothing at all to do with—with what happened."

"Good."

She blew her nose again. "Suppose—I mean, just for the sake of argument, that you'd asked a girl you—well, you thought you liked to go out and celebrate your birthday with you."

"An agreeable supposition," he prompted.

"And—and anyway, she wasn't feeling any too well but she went because she didn't want to spoil your party. And then when she got inside the restaurant and smelled the food, she had to go out and—and embarrass you."

"She would not embarrass me," said Rhys. "She would distress me."

"Then—then what would you do?"

He shrugged. "The best I could, I suppose. How sick would she be, for the sake, as you say, of argument?"

"Sick enough to have to go to the hospital. I mean—you wouldn't flounce off in a snit and leave her to go by herself?"

"My God, no!"

"And you'd maybe send her some flowers or something when you found out she'd had to have her appendix out?"

"I'd probably be camping on the doormat outside her room and driving the nurses crazy till they let me go inside. How would you expect any man to act?"

"Sometimes people don't get what they expect." Janet had hold of herself now. "I don't know why I brought that up. Just trying to get my mind off this other business, I suppose."

A Mountie is not so easily beguiled. Somewhere, and Rhys would track him down or hand in his badge, existed a cad who required to be dealt with as The Right Honorable Mr. Trudeau had once so tersely and feistily offered to deal with an Honorable Member of the Opposition. Only he did not say so, for such language should not be used in front of a lady.

"And you say Gilly and Elmer and Bobby are all three gone? That little kid!"

"Now, Janet," said Rhys, "surely you cannot believe that Elmer Bain would harm Gilly or her son?"

"Stranger things have happened. Anyway, what if they're not all together? What if somebody started to take Gilly and Bobby away somewhere, and Elmer went chasing after them? What if he got killed like Dot, and his body dumped in the woods somewhere? How do we know they're not all three dead by now?"

Rhys felt a powerful impulse to exercise a greater degree of tact than was consistent with departmental regulations. He'd better get out of here and put his mind back on his job.

"My dear Janet, you must not let yourself get worked up over something that most likely hasn't happened. Why don't you go over to the Mansion and give Marion a hand, eh? Let me do the worrying. That's what I get paid for."

She blew her altogether delectable nose again. "All right, I suppose I ought to see what's happening. I expect I'll find her trying to make coffee on the waffle iron. Where will you be in case any of us need to get hold of you?"

He thought it would be a splendid idea if she personally wanted to, but he did not say so. "First I am going to be right here for a while, if you don't mind, running up a terrible phone bill, which will not be charged to your brother. Then I shall take a run out to Jason Bain's house if you'll tell me how to find it. Elmer may possibly have taken Gilly and Bobby there for safety's sake, you know."

"I never thought of that." Nor did Janet think much of the suggestion now, Rhys could see. However, she drew him a neat map, gave him careful directions to go with it, and then began wrapping up the leftover doughnuts to take over to Marion.

He worked off some of his excess tact by scrubbing Janet's frying pans for her, saw her safely to the door of the Mansion with her burden of provender, then went to the telephone. The information he asked for was buried deep in time and, no doubt, dust. He persevered, and got it at last. The facts were pretty much as he'd expected. He took meticulous notes, thanked the exhausted-sounding voice at the other end of the wire, and hung up. At last he took his neat little map in hand and went to call on Jason Bain.

The road out to Bain's lair was as brutal as Janet had warned him it would be. He bumped along over ancient ruts and fallen logs, offering up pious utterances to whichever deity was in charge of automobile springs. Perhaps these were heard. In any event, he was agreeably surprised to reach his destination with the car still more or less intact.

That he had in fact got to where he intended was indisputable. "You'll know the place when you see it," Janet had explained, "because the town dump's out the other way."

The house itself was not a great eyesore, being merely a smallish two-story dwelling of no particular style, in reasonable repair. Its clapboards were fresh-painted on two sides and part of a third in a strange greenish-bronze shade that had no doubt been arrived at by thriftily blending together whatever odds and ends of paint had happened to be lying around. Here was a proof of Elmer's industry, though hardly a testimonial to his eye for color.

Jason Bain's notion of landscaping was even more wildly original than his son's of decorating. The yard was one magnificent scramble of broken-down farm machinery, threadbare airplane tires, old lumber, *objets trouvés* of all descriptions and a good many that were indescribable. In the midst of this welter stood the old man, being monarch of all he surveyed. It had to be Bain, since Rhys couldn't imagine anybody else would care to reign here. As the car pulled up toward the house, he ambled over.

"Morning, Mr. Bain," the Mountie called out. "Is your son here?"

"No, he ain't," snapped the squire. "What you want him for, eh?"

"I want him for questioning, about a murder and a possible kidnaping. Perhaps I should explain that I'm Detective Inspector Rhys of the Royal Canadian Mounted Police."

The old man backed away, yellow fangs bared in his bony, unshaven jaw. "I ain't puttin' up one red cent for lawyer fees."

"Nobody's asked you to, so far as I know. I merely want to talk to Elmer. Where is he?"

"How'm I s'posed to know? I ain't seen 'im since—" Bain did a rapid switch. "Who's been murdered?"

"A local woman named Dorothy Fewter. Do you know her?"

"Black-haired slut that was Sam Neddick's fancy piece. What's she got to do with Elmer?"

"It's departmental procedure for us to ask the questions and for you to answer," Rhys reminded him gently. "You were about to tell me when and where you last saw your son, I believe?"

"Day Henry Druffitt was buried," the father admitted grudgingly. "'Round maybe three o'clock in the afternoon."

"And where was this?"

"At the Mansion."

"What were you doing there?"

"Man's got a right to call on his own son, ain't he? Maybe I got lonesome." The ocher teeth bared again in an unlovely smile.

"I should prefer you to be more specific," said Rhys.

"Don't know's I'm obliged to be if I don't choose, not unless you serve papers on me. I had some private business to talk over with 'im, that's all."

"To the best of your knowledge, was anybody else present at this—er—conversation?"

"Just said it was private, didn't I? They was all down to the funeral, far as I know."

"Why didn't you go, too?"

Bain shrugged. "Hank Druffitt was nothin' to me."

"Then your statement is that you went to the Treadway house, commonly referred to as the Mansion, for the specific purpose of discussing a confidential business matter with your son."

"Put it that way if you want to."

"This discussion was entirely amicable and—er—businesslike?"

"It was."

"Then perhaps, Mr. Bain," said Rhys plaintively, "you might explain to me why an eyewitness has testified that your son caught you alone inside the house when he returned early from the funeral, that there was a violent argument during which he accused you of breaking and entering with felonious intent, and that he threw you out the door."

CHAPTER 18

"What witness?" roared Bain.

"Oh, we have to save a few surprises for the trial."

"Whose trial you talkin' about?"

A Mountie is forbidden to threaten a suspect. Rhys merely scratched his red mustache and cocked a dark brown eyebrow. "Now, Mr. Bain, perhaps you'd care to go over your statement with me once more. You say you arrived at the Mansion on the afternoon of the funeral. You knew of course that Marion Emery is a cousin of the Druffitts, and that Gilly Bascom is their daughter. It stood to reason they'd be down at the church. Sam Neddick, your friend, must also have told you that Bert Wadman would be marching with the Owls, and that he himself would be serving as the undertaker's assistant. Would you care to comment on these facts?"

Bain did not care to comment.

"Very well, then we may take them as stated. Now, since your son has a car and the ladies he's boarding with do not, it would be reasonable to assume that he might be driving them down to the village and staying for the funeral so he could bring them back. In fact, Elmer did take Gilly and her son, as well as Marion Emery, down to the village and then come back for Janet Wadman and Dot Fewter. If you had really intended to have an important private business conference with him, you could easily enough have telephoned in advance to tell him to return to the Mansion while the others were away. That is a telephone wire I see up there, is it not?"

Bain didn't answer.

"Therefore, we have to deduce that no such conference was intended and that what you really had in mind was a spot of trespass. Your son came home early because one of his passengers wasn't feeling well, and caught you in the act. The amicable discussion you alluded to was in fact a flaming row. Have we got it straight now?"

Apparently they had. Under its overgrowth of gray stubble, Bain's face was the color of old brick. "Damned ingrate! Turned on 'is own father like a she-bear with a sore backside."

"What were you two fighting about, other than the fact that he'd caught you where you had no business to be?"

"Didn't your star witness tell you that?" sneered the miscreant.

"I'd rather you told me yourself. It will look better on your record if you co-operate, you know."

Bain swallowed. "All right, if that's the way you want to put it. I got nothin' to be ashamed of. I was lookin' for a patent which is my own rightful property."

"Why is it your rightful property?"

"Because me an' Charles Treadway was in business together an' I can prove it. Accordin' to our agreement, his wife held the patent right long as she lived. Soon as she died, it passed to me an' I been tryin' to get it. Marion Emery's been holdin' out on me, claimin' she couldn't find it. I got sore an' decided to take matters into my own hands, that's all. Can't blame a man for wantin' what's his."

"But you did not take the patent from the Mansion?"

"I did not."

"Would you have done so if Elmer hadn't interrupted your search?"

"You can't hold me accountable for what I might or might not o' done. Maybe I'd o' called you in to make Miz Emery fork it over. You're s'posed to stick up for law an' order, ain't you?"

"Well put, Mr. Bain. You've been creating quite a stir about that patent, by and large, have you not?"

"A man's got a right to his own property."

"Considering your liberal views regarding the act of trespass, I'm surprised you take such a vehement stand on that issue. When did you learn the patent had been found?"

A crafty smirk flitted across the unlovely features. "I ain't learned yet, exactly."

"What do you mean, 'exactly'?"

"Anybody thinks they can put one over on me—"

"Are you referring to Marion Emery or Elizabeth Druffitt?"

Bain hunched his shoulders and shut his mouth.

"Which of the two was it," said Rhys gently, "that you thought you'd killed last night?"

This was clearly one question Bain hadn't bargained for. "Wait a minute," he stammered. "Hold on there! What you drivin' at?"

"I told you when I arrived that Dorothy Fewter had been murdered," the Mountie reminded him. "You didn't ask me when she died, or where or how. I thought perhaps it might be because you already knew."

"You told me not to ask no questions! I—why should I, anyways? It's no business o' mine."

"That's rather a detached attitude for a man in your position, isn't it? Very well, then, although you still haven't asked, I'll tell you. Miss Fewter was killed by being hit over the head with a rock sometime shortly after midnight on the Treadway place. She was wearing a dress which until that same afternoon had belonged to Mrs. Elizabeth Druffitt. Since Mrs. Druffitt has a reputation for never giving anything away, and since Miss Fewter bore a striking resemblance to both Mrs. Druffitt and Miss Emery, it's been suggested that the dress fooled the murderer into mistaking her for one of the other two in the dark. Since you've already been caught trespassing at the Mansion once and since you've expressed such determination to get your patent back, you must surely realize what sort of position that leaves you in."

"I damn well don't," Bain snarled back.

"Then suppose we examine the situation a little further. You've paid at least two visits to the Druffitt house since Dr. Druffitt's death. Is that correct?"

"Just two," Bain mumbled.

"Thank you. On both occasions, Marion Emery was present as well as Elizabeth Druffitt. On the second occasion, you were seen leaving the house looking, as a witness put it, like the cat that swallowed the canary. You've just now intimated that somebody is trying to put something over on you regarding the patent, so we can assume the person to whom you refer is either Marion Emery or Mrs. Druffitt, or possibly the pair of them working in collusion. Do you follow me so far?"

Bain's Adam's apple made a couple of quick trips up and down his skinny throat.

"Good," said Rhys. "You see how neatly everything fits together. Now, a prosecuting attorney might take the angle that having failed in your first raid on the Mansion and being by now convinced a scheme was afoot to trick you out of your property, you attempted a second raid under cover of darkness. Perhaps you knew your son was taking Gilly Bascom out for the evening."

"I never!"

"In any event, you, being a sensible man, would have waited till you thought everybody was either away or asleep. You would therefore have been startled when you met a woman on the lawn who looked like one of those you believed to be plotting against you. You might have become enraged, as you were seen to do on the previous occasion. You might have been alarmed at being caught trespassing again. In either case it would have been reprehensible but not unnatural for you to strike out at the woman with the first weapon that came to hand. As it happens, she was struck on top of the head. She was a tall woman, but you are taller. Would you care to save us a lot of bother and make a confession?"

"No! I never! You got no case against me. It's all guesswork. I was right here in my own bed."

"Can you prove it?"

A cornered rat will fight. Bain's eyes began to show as yellow as his teeth. "If you're fixin' to pin somethin' on me, why'd you come here askin' for Elmer?"

"Because Elmer is nowhere to be found and it's quite possible, you know, that he disappeared in order to avoid being questioned. Even if you two are really on the outs and not just doing an act for the neighbors' benefit, he may not care for the idea of testifying against his own father in a murder case. I must say Elmer struck me as a decent sort of chap, all things considered."

"The hell he is," snorted Bain. After that he didn't say any more for quite a while. Rhys waited like a cat at a mousehole. At last the rat went away and the mouse came out. "You claim I killed the woman to get hold o' the patent, right?"

"I offered a hypothesis built on the evidence."

"Then you can take your goddamn hypothesis an' stuff it, Mountie. Your argument ain't worth the powder to blow it to hell, 'cause neither is that patent!"

Bain thought he was hurling a bombshell, but it proved to be a dud. Rhys merely nodded.

"I know. I've been in touch with the patent office. The rights expired some years ago, and it was a silly idea in the first place. Miss Emery showed it to me. I can think of only one really good use you could have put that patent to. It made a fine red herring."

"Huh?"

"Oh yes, Mr. Bain. You hung onto those papers because you're a very far-seeing man. When Elmer caught you in the Mansion, you weren't looking for the patent. You were putting it where it could be found, weren't you? *Precious Bane* must have tickled your sense of humor, eh? You were a bit too clever there. Nobody spotted it for almost an hour."

Bain couldn't keep his lips from twitching in a sneer of contempt that was as good as a confession. Sure of his man now, Rhys went on.

"All those threats and outcries about your rights served their purpose. You managed to convince Marion Emery and Elizabeth Druffitt that the patent must be of great value.

Your plan was to work yourself neatly into a corner and let them force you to buy them out. After loud cries and protestations, you would part with a considerable sum of money. Miss Emery would sign over her rights in the patent to you, and Mrs. Druffitt would force her daughter to do likewise, which I daresay Gilly would be glad enough to do anyway, eh? They wouldn't know it till you served them with a court order to hand over the deeds, but they'd also be signing away their interests in Mrs. Treadway's estate."

"That's hogwash!"

"No, it's not, Mr. Bain. You knew that to them, as to everybody else but yourself, Treadway Enterprises Ltd was a joke that had gone stale long ago. In fact, it's still very much a going concern, according to provincial records. My information is that you and Charles Treadway formed a partnership. You put up five hundred dollars, which I'm sure you've managed to get back somehow, and Treadway, being long on enthusiasm but by then short of ready cash, pledged the deeds to his house and land as capital. That is correct, eh?"

Bain couldn't very well say it wasn't, so he said nothing.

"Your partner meant to redeem the deeds, no doubt, as soon as his dreams of affluence came true, but he died in what we must now assume for want of proof was a freak accident. Does it mean anything to you that his wife died in essentially the same way?"

"Not a damn thing!" spat Bain.

"You never did explain to her about the partnership, did you? At Treadway's death, his interest in the company reverted to his wife, but she seems not to have understood what that implied. I'm told she once negotiated with a builder to sell off part of the land. She couldn't legally have sold anything without your being an equal party to the deal, and I'm sure you were looking forward to telling her so when you got the chance. However, that deal fell through, so you had to cook up another one. How much have you paid for the patent?"

"Nothin'."

"I see. You'd hooked your fish and you thought you could take your time about pulling them in. Too bad. I can't think of anyone I'd rather arrest for swindling. What were your plans for the property, Mr. Bain? You know it's no good for farming or building."

Bain wasn't saying.

"No matter," said Rhys, "I can guess. You've no doubt been thinking of the tourists. With this new road and the fad for campgrounds, it might work, at that, except that you'd have to trek your campers across Bert Wadman's property to get them to your pond and he'd never allow that."

Bain's penchant for legal quibbles got the better of his caution. "He couldn't stop me! There's a right o' way."

"Is there, now?" Rhys nodded, perfectly satisfied with the result of his expedition. "Thank you, Mr. Bain. And if you get any more bright ideas, such as leaving town without my permission, I suggest you keep them to yourself."

CHAPTER 19

Rhys realized he'd been a bit free in his remarks to Bain. The damnable thing was, the man, repulsive snake-in-the-grass though he might be, hadn't actually done anything illegal except a spot of trespass, which he could always wiggle out of on the pretense that he'd come to see his son.

Even if Bain had managed to swindle Marion and Gilly out of their inheritance he'd have been acting within the framework of the law because he'd maneuvered Marion and her cousin into initiating the deal. One couldn't very well arrest him on a charge of attempted larceny of Janet Wadman's pet snapping turtles. One couldn't even give him a richly deserved poke in the mouth without violating the code of the Force. As Rhys drove back over the all-but-impassable road he felt there were times when a policeman's lot was not, in sooth, a happy one.

At least the snapping turtles were safe for the nonce, but what about the people? Was Gilly Bascom alive or dead? Perhaps he should be asking himself, was she a victim or was she the killer? Why couldn't it have been she and not her son who threw that rock, and why couldn't she have aimed to hit either the mother she couldn't get on with or the coheiress she could do better without?

Why couldn't Elmer have seen her do it and have had to be killed, too? She and Bobby between them might have been able to get his body into his car and take it away somewhere to hide. That was the trouble with murdering. No doubt there were lots of people who'd done one quiet little job—hidden Grandpa's pills, perhaps, when Grandpa was having one of his spells—and got away with it and never felt the urge to try again. But all too often, one led to another.

By this time, Dot Fewter's body should be down at Ben Potts's place, and headquarters have sent someone out to have a look at it. Rhys wondered if Olson had thought to notify the mother before she got word of the tragedy via the grapevine. He should have done that himself.

One way or another, the news must have gotten around. As he neared the undertaking parlor, Rhys could see, buzzing around the door, a group of shocked villagers, unready to believe what they hadn't yet seen. A pudgy man in a black suit who must be Potts was doing his futile best to keep order without antagonizing any of his future customers.

"Folks, you've got to be reasonable," he was protesting as Rhys parked the car and walked over to the group. "Fred Olson gave me strict orders that nobody's to be let in till official permission's been given. I'm sorry, Mabel, but if I said yes to one, the rest would—yes, I know you were, but—"

Somehow or other, Rhys melted through the crowd and got to Potts's side. The buzzing stopped even before he held up his hand for silence.

"Mr. Potts is acting in accordance with rules and regulations, ladies and gentlemen. The examination is only a formality, but it must be done. After that, Mr. Potts will have his own professional duties to perform. Once they are completed, no doubt the late Miss Fewter's family will wish to receive your kind condolences in the usual manner. Will they not, Mr. Potts?"

Mr. Potts was of the opinion that they would. He estimated that he could complete his professional duties by late afternoon.

"Thank you, Mr. Potts," said Rhys. "At that time, we shall hope also to have an official statement for you, since I expect Miss Fewter's friends and relatives are deeply concerned as to how this dreadful thing could have happened. Until then, I'm afraid I shan't be in a position to answer any questions. It will greatly assist our investigation if you'll all go about your accustomed daily affairs until Mr. Potts has things in readiness for your reception. Thank you for your excellent co-operation."

He gave them a deferential little bow, then got himself and Potts neatly inside before the people outside had time to make up their minds whether they cared to co-operate or not. A sodden bundle of old clothes got up and waddled toward them.

Mrs. Fewter's voice was choked with sobs, but the words came out clear enough.

"Have you caught the murderin' devil yet?"

"Not yet, Mrs. Fewter," Rhys answered gently. "We shall, you know."

"I know. The Mounties always get their man. But that won't bring my Dottie back to me."

Tears overflowed the puffs of fat around the woman's eyes and splashed down her rusty black front. Although the morning was warm, she had an old winter coat huddled around her. Feeling chilled from the shock, no doubt. She ought to have something hot to drink. Unappetizing sight though she was, Rhys felt an aching pity for the bereft mother.

"Mrs. Fewter, do you have any thoughts at all about why anyone would want to kill your daughter?"

"No. Who'd want to do a thing like that? She never hurt a fly. It must o' been one o' them sex maniacs, is all I can think of. Was she—?"

"Oh no, please put your mind at rest on that score. Somebody appears to have hit her over the head with a rock and simply left her lying where she fell. It may have been an accident. In any event, I'm sure she never knew what struck her, if that's any comfort to you."

Mrs. Fewter sniffled into a tissue Ben Potts pressed into her hand. "It's so awful," she whispered. "I can't think straight."

"You and your daughter got along pretty well, did you?"

"Oh lordy, yes. Dottie was always good to me no matter what. I never raised but the two, and first my Joe gets killed on that darned old motorbike, and now this! It ain't right. I don't care what you say, it ain't right."

"Nobody said it was, Mrs. Fewter," said Rhys. "Mr. Potts, I wonder if you might be able to find a cup of hot tea or coffee for this lady, eh? I think she could use it. Plenty of sugar, please."

While Potts was off getting this excellent remedy for the shock Mrs. Fewter was undoubtedly suffering from, the doctor from headquarters arrived. His diagnosis was exactly what Rhys had expected. Dot had been instantly killed by a hard blow on the crown of the head. As the rock showed traces of blood and hair and fitted the wound, it could safely be called the murder weapon. There was no other physical injury. As for the question of molestation, the doctor could only say that the victim had been engaged shortly before her demise in an activity which, fortunately for Mrs. Fewter's sensibilities, he described in words she would not be likely to understand.

"Yes, that is correct," said Rhys. "It fits in with the testimony we have and cannot be considered an abnormal circumstance. And the time of death?"

"I should say somewhere around midnight, on the visible evidence."

"That will do well enough, thank you, Doctor."

Rhys helped the doctor make his way through the crowd to his car, then came back inside.

"Would you care to view the remains yourself, Inspector, before I get to work?" Potts offered.

"I think not, thank you."

"Go ahead if you want to," Mrs. Fewter sniffled. "Don't hold back on account o' me."

She sniffled again. "Dot come home an' showed me them clothes Miz Druffitt give 'er before she went on up to the Wadmans'. I says, 'They're real nice but where do you think you'll ever get a chance to wear 'em, eh? I'll find places,' she says real saucy an' she put 'em back in 'er grip on top of 'er nightgownd. So then I knew she was settin' her cap for Elmer Bain."

"Was she, indeed? And why might your daughter be doing that, Mrs. Fewter?"

"That's kind of a dumb question if you don't mind me sayin' so, Inspector. Why would any woman go after a man that's earnin' good money, eh? 'Cause she was sick an' tired o' scrubbin' other people's floors, that's why."

"But I thought it was common knowledge around town that Elmer is—er—interested elsewhere."

"Huh!" Back on the familiar ground of local gossip, Mrs. Fewter began to look almost human. "If you think Elizabeth Druffitt's goin' to stand for Gilly marryin' a Bain, you got another think comin', mister. Dot told me so herself, sittin' right there at our kitchen table. She always had a snack soon as she come home from the Druffitts'. I'd have somethin' she liked all ready an' waitin' an' the teapot keepin' hot on the back o' the stove. Lord ha' mercy, the house is goin' to feel empty without 'er!"

She mopped at her eyes with the disintegrated wad of tissue. "Dot says to me—was it only yesterday afternoon? Mighty Jehu, it feels like a million years! As I started to say, she come back to show me the dress an' all, an' get 'er nightgownd, not but what she couldn't o' slept in 'er petticoat for one night but she was hopin' Janet would ast 'er to stay on a few days longer. She says she never et so good in 'er life, an' Janet talkin' so nice an' makin' her take the biggest piece just as if she was comp'ny."

Mrs. Fewter blew her nose again. "An' then o' course with Elmer right next door, not that a Bain's anythin' to write home about but the old man's got money or ought to have, the Lord knows, an' Elmer's worked up to be foreman down at the lumber mill. I never heard anythin' against Elmer, far's that goes. Keeps 'imself to hisself, but you can't hang a man for that, can you? An' Dot's goin' to be thirty-four her next birthday. No, she ain't, is she? I keep forgettin'."

Perhaps it was cruel to keep badgering the heartbroken mother with questions, but Rhys had to do it. "Exactly what was it your daughter told you about Gilly Bascom and Elmer Bain, Mrs. Fewter?"

"Sittin' right there at the kitchen table she was, drinkin' a cup o' tea an' eatin' one o' them cimmamon buns she liked. 'I wisht you could taste Janet Wadman's doughnuts, Ma,' she says. 'I'll try to sneak you a couple in my grip when I come back.' So then she told me how Gilly took at Miz Druffitt after the funeral for actin' so spiteful to Elmer comin' out o' the church, which I didn't happen to see myself but you can bet there was plenty o' talk about it afterward. You wasn't there, was you?"

"No, but I heard the story from Janet Wadman. And what did Mrs. Druffitt reply to her daughter?"

"Dot says Miz Druffitt got real mad an' says Gilly needn't go gettin' any foolish notions about Elmer Bain 'cause she wouldn't stand for Gilly lowerin' herself an' the family no more'n what she already done, runnin' off with that Bob Bascom. I guess I don't have to tell you about that, eh?"

"No, you don't," said Rhys hastily. "Please go on with what you were saying."

"Well, anyways, Miz Druffitt says Elmer's father was no better'n a common thief, tryin' to do Gilly out o' that patent of Uncle Charles's that was worth a fortune like as not an' if she didn't have no shame she might at least show a little common sense. So then Gilly started bawlin' an' yellin' an' says she didn't care what the old man done, her mother hadn't no call to act so mean to Elmer."

Mrs. Fewter had perked up a good deal. She had a story to tell and a willing audience to tell it to. The artist can forget his private woe in the expression of his art. "So her mother says back real sweet like she does that Gilly was no judge o' men, which is true enough on the face of it, I guess, though Bob Bascom never had a chance with them so down on 'im right from the start not that he was much to start with. But I wouldn't o' kept throwin' Bob up to Gilly myself, not if she was my daughter." She was a mother again. She reached for more tissues.

"And then what happened?" Rhys insisted.

"Well, I guess Gilly started in about Elmer again, an' Miz Druffitt says, 'That's enough, Gillian. You've made one mistake and that's enough. If you marry Elmer Bain, it will be over my dead body."

"Did she, now? Thank you, Mrs. Fewter. Thank you very much indeed."

CHAPTER 20

Rhys took Mrs. Fewter back to her scabrous home and found a kind neighbor waiting to fix her lunch and help her get ready for the visiting hours at the funeral parlor. After that, he couldn't think of anything to do but go back to the Mansion and wait. He wasn't surprised to run into a great deal of traffic on the normally quiet hill road. Human nature abounded in Pitcherville as elsewhere, and if it was not possible to get a look at the corpse, the next best move for the sensation seekers was to view the spot where it had lain.

He wormed his way through the stream of cars as best he could and pulled into the drive. Fred Olson was out there with a shotgun cradled in his massive arms, trying to maintain law and order and ignore the smart cracks from passing vehicles. Rhys told him to keep up the good work, and went inside.

As Rhys had hoped, Janet Wadman was there, trying to beguile the waiting by giving Marion a cooking lesson, doing all the work herself while the older woman looked on, not even pretending to be interested. They both pounced on him.

"Any news, Madoc?"

"The Mounties have not yet got their man, if that's what you mean. Has there been a telephone message for me?"

"No, the phone hasn't rung once," said Marion. "Don't ask me why. I'd expected every snoop in town to be on the line by now."

"I anticipated that possibility myself," he explained. "That is why I've asked that no local calls be put through. I want the line free in case Gilly or Elmer tries to get in touch. How is Mrs. Druffitt?"

"Still asleep, thank God. She seems all right. I looked in on her a few minutes ago."

"Have you had anything to eat, Madoc? Can I make you a cup of tea?" Janet, looking charmingly useless in her pink sundress and fresh bandage, was probably the clearest head among them.

"Thank you," Rhys said with a wistful smile. "I'd like that. Perhaps someone might take a cup out to Olson, too. He looks as if he could use a small act of kindness about now."

"I'll do it," Marion volunteered. "Might as well let the peanut gallery get a look at the next victim." She picked up the mug Janet filled and took it out the side door.

"Do you think Marion honestly believes Dot Fewter was killed in mistake for her?" Rhys asked Janet.

"That's hard to say," she replied, doing a neat one-handed job with the teapot. "Marion's afraid of something, that's for sure, but I'm more inclined to think it's you. I think she really expected to be arrested, and the only thing that's saved her so far is this strange disappearance of Gilly and Elmer and Bobby. I think what she's mainly scared of is that if they turn up safe and sound and innocent, you'll clap the handcuffs on her. You won't, will you?"

How could any man have walked away from anything so lovely? Decidedly, Pierre Trudeau had known whereof he spoke. "You don't want it to be anybody, do you?" he teased. "Would you settle for wicked trolls?"

"It's all very well for you to joke! You're only doing your job. But what's it going to be like for me, eh, knowing I've helped to get somebody convicted of murder?"

Her lips quivered. Rhys shoved his hands deep in his pockets and reminded himself fiercely that he was on duty. "Shall we worry about that when we get a conviction, Janet?"

She dabbed at her flushed cheeks with the back of her bandage. "All right, Madoc, I'm sorry. I'd better tend to my biscuits, hadn't I, and leave the rest of it to you. There's not one solitary bite to eat in this house, and Marion doesn't even seem to care. Can't blame her, I suppose. I meant for her to roll them out because I can't manage the rolling pin, but she's out there chewing the fat with Fred so I might as well make drop biscuits."

She began scooping up neat spoonfuls of dough and plopping them on a greased cookie sheet. "Still and all, with a growing boy in the house, you'd think—Madoc, surely nothing's happened to Bobby, has it?"

"Janet, to tell you the plain truth, I don't know. I'm going out and relieve Olson for a while. You'd better go over and get Bert's dinner. Maybe you could bring back a few sandwiches or something if the place is that short of grub."

"Yes, of course. Tell Marion to keep an eye on those biscuits, eh? She ought to be able to manage that much, anyway."

She flashed her dimples, and he turned and fled from temptation. He then spent a tedious hour or so waving his arms and shouting at motorists to keep moving. After a while, word must have got around that there was really nothing to see. The line dwindled, then evaporated.

Rhys went back into the house, found Marion and Olson playing euchre, kibitzed a minute or two, wandered into the library and noted that Mrs. Druffitt was still peacefully asleep, phoned headquarters and learned as he'd expected that the road patrol had not picked up Bain's car yet, went back to the kitchen and ate a few of Janet's biscuits, which Marion had let get much too brown, phoned Ben Potts for no particular reason, then cut the undertaker short in case his own colleagues might be trying to reach the Mansion.

Janet came back about one o'clock with a basketful of sandwiches and fresh vegetables. After giving Marion a few terse words on the subject of overdone biscuits she brewed a pot of tea and fed the rest their lunch. She made Marion clear up, showing great force of character, then let herself be talked into a game of euchre. She was holding high trumps, awkwardly because of her bandaged hand, when the call came through. When Rhys came back from talking into the phone, her cards were lying face up and unheeded on the table.

"Did they—is Bobby—"

"Bobby's fine and so are the others," Rhys reassured her. "They were picked up at a restaurant in Moncton, eating chicken and ice cream. They're on the way back here now."

Marion and the marshal broke in with excited questions. Their raised voices at last woke Elizabeth Druffitt. She appeared in the doorway looking only a little bit less immaculate than usual, but with dark-purple half moons under her eyes.

"It's okay, Elizabeth," Marion shouted. "They've been found and they're coming back."

Mrs. Druffitt wheeled on Rhys. "Have you arrested him?"

"Whom would you mean, Mrs. Druffitt?"

"Elmer Bain, of course. The man who tried to murder me."

"Why, no. You see, he is not here yet," Rhys reminded her gently. "In any case we are not allowed to arrest anybody unless we can lay a charge against him."

"But I've just told you—"

"Ah but you see telling is not quite good enough. There is that troublesome business of having to present evidence."

She started to say something more, then clamped her lips together and glared. Janet got up from the table. "Let me get you a cup of tea, Mrs. Druffitt."

"No, thank you. I couldn't touch a thing." Nevertheless she drank the tea and ate several of the overbrowned biscuits with it.

Janet, glad of something to do, hovered at her elbow refilling the teacup and offering to scramble some eggs. "You must be famished. I'll bet you haven't had a bite to eat since yesterday."

"Probably not. I don't remember. I'm much too upset. When a public servant refuses to do his clear and simple duty—" She continued to glare at Rhys until she had the satisfaction of seeing him turn red and begin to nibble at the left-hand corner of his mustache. Then she turned on Marion.

"Can't you do something about this dreadful kitchen?

What if somebody were to come in? I hate to think what people would say if they could see this beautiful old family home turned into a gambling saloon."

"Don't be funny, Elizabeth," said her cousin. "You know damn well Aunt Aggie used to sit here playing high-low-jack with Sam Neddick for a penny a point about five nights out of the week. You're a hell of a one to talk about gambling in the first place, considering how Henry spent his time whenever he managed to get off the leash."

"At least my husband didn't go chasing after every skirt in town."

"Damn right he didn't. The woman he had was one too many for him as it was. And if you're trying to get at me about my old man, let me remind you that he at least knew which sex was which. Don't think everybody wasn't wise to what your dear, saintly father tried to teach those boys in his Sunday-school class."

With deliberate offensiveness, Marion stubbed out her cigarette in the already overflowing ashtray, scooped up the scattered cards, and began dealing a euchre hand. Elizabeth Druffitt sniffed, gathered together the remains of her dignity, and went back to the library. Janet touched Rhys diffidently on the coat sleeve.

"I hope you didn't mind what she said about not doing your duty."

"No, my dear—cousin."

"Anybody else would have at least said, 'Thank you for getting Gilly and Bobby back safely.'"

"One must take people as they are. Would there be another cup of tea?" He'd have preferred a little more sympathy, but he couldn't risk having Mrs. Druffitt suddenly reappear and report him for lewd and lascivious behavior.

It was almost five o'clock and Janet was beginning to worry out loud about Bert's supper when a caravan at last pulled into the yard. Elmer's green Ford was first, then a police car, then a delegation of sports from the village tagging along to see what was up. The uniformed Mountie who had been driving the second car got out and escorted the runaways into the Mansion.

"Afternoon, Inspector. These the people you've been looking for?"

"Yes, indeed. Thank you, Sergeant. Stick around, will you? I may have a passenger for you to take back."

Marion, Janet, and even Mrs. Druffitt pressed close behind him, craning over his shoulder for a closer look as the group entered the kitchen. Elmer towered in the middle, one arm around Gilly's narrow shoulders and the other great paw engulfing Bobby's hand. All three looked confused, exhausted, bedraggled, and blissful. Gilly had the remains of a purple orchid pinned to her black dress and was holding her left hand out in front of her like a talisman. On the last finger but one was a shiny new yellow-gold wedding band.

"Gillian!" screamed her mother. "What have you done?"

Elmer gaped at Elizabeth Druffitt. "You? I thought—"

"You thought you'd killed me, you murdering devil!"

"Killed you, nothin'," he yelled back. "You was already dead. I seen you in the headlights last night when I drove up to the house. You was layin' on the grass, right over there." He pointed out the window to the spot where Dot Fewter's body had been found. "I got out an' felt your hand. It was ice cold and I couldn't find no pulse. Then I touched your head an' got blood on my hand so I knew you must be dead. I washed off the blood at the outside faucet so's Gilly wouldn't see it an' I backed the car up so's Gilly wouldn't see you, neither."

"How could she help seeing?"

"She was asleep! She fell asleep at the drive-in an' slept all the way back. So then I woke 'er up an' says, 'Gilly, we're leavin'.' An' she says, 'I got to take Bobby,' an' I says, 'Sure.' So we got 'im an' we went." The young giant took a tighter grip on his new wife, folded the other arm around his stepson, and glared defiance at them all.

"You're lying!" Mrs. Druffitt shrieked. "Gillian would never have gone off and left her own mother—or what she thought was her mother—dead in the dooryard. You tricked her! You drugged her!"

"I told you she never seen nothin'," Elmer insisted. "We went in the front door an' she waited downstairs while I snuck up an' got Bobby."

"Is that true, Gilly?" said Rhys.

"Yes," she shouted back.

"What did you do while Elmer was upstairs?"

"Came out here to the kitchen and put what was left of the cookies and milk in a paper bag and made a couple of peanut-butter sandwiches because I knew he'd be hungry when he woke up. I didn't know where we were going or if there'd be anything to eat there."

"Did you happen to look out the window?"

"No, I was in too big a hurry. Anyway, I'd put the light on so I could see to fix the sandwiches. If I had looked up, I wouldn't have been able to see out."

"Didn't you ask Elmer what this—er—sudden excursion was all about?"

"No. Why should I? I knew we were going to do it sooner or later anyway."

"I see. How long would you say you were in the house?"

"Not more than a minute or two, I shouldn't think. Elmer just rolled Bobby in a blanket and brought him downstairs still asleep. He didn't even bring anything for him to wear, the big dope." She gave the big dope a glance of unutterable adoration. "We had to stop at a store somewhere and buy Bobby those clothes he's got on."

"So then you went back out the front door and got into the car and drove off?"

"That's right," said Elmer. "An' Gilly never seen a thing."

"Do you have any idea what time it was when you left?"

"Half-past one," said Gilly. "I remember glancing at the clock as I was reaching for the peanut butter. I was surprised it was so late. But of course we'd stayed at the drive-in for a while after the show was over. Just—talking. You see, we'd already bought the license."

Mrs. Druffitt made a queer, strangling noise.

"But what did happen to you, Mama?" said Gilly. "Did you fall, or what? Are you all right now?"

"I'm surprised you even bother to ask," sniffed her mother.

"She was dead," Elmer insisted. "I wouldn't o' gone off if there was anything we could o' done to help. But I could see right away it was no accident, an' what with Gilly's Aunt Aggie an' her father dyin' like that one right on top o' the other I had a pretty shrewd idea what the Mounties was doin' up here. I wasn't havin' Gilly mixed up in no more murders. But how—"

"It was Dorothy Fewter you saw," Rhys explained. "She happened to be wearing," his mustache twitched, "one of your mother-in-law's dresses."

"Then how could he know?" said the new Mrs. Bain. "Black dresses all look alike in the dark, don't they?"

"It wasn't black," said Elmer doggedly. "It was that same dress she had on the night she told me I couldn't take you to the high-school dance an' slammed the door in my face. Would I be likely ever to forget what that one looked like, eh?"

"But Mama wouldn't have been wearing a light-colored dress last night, honey. She's in mourning for Daddy."

"Grandma says she ain't going to wear anything but solid black for a whole year," Bobby piped up.

"Don't say 'ain't,'" his grandmother reproved automatically.

"Pop says it."

"Pop!" Mrs. Druffitt went totally out of control. "Pop! My God in Heaven, Gillian, have you no sense of shame at all? First that Bascom creature and now this—this Bain! How could you be so heartless, after all I've done for you?"

Rhys gazed at the raging, trembling woman, light dawning at last in his sad, bloodhound eyes. "You have a very strong sense of duty, have you not, Mrs. Druffitt?"

"I hope I know what's right!"

"Did you really think it was right to kill three people because you didn't care for the house your daughter was living in?"

The July sun beamed down on the dry grass where old Aggie Treadway's hired girl had lain dead the night before. A flock of sparrows twittered down, trim in their patterned uniforms of brown and beige, then whirled away. Inside the kitchen, nobody noticed. Nobody spoke. Nobody moved, until at last Marion Emery broke the silence.

"So it was you, Elizabeth." She didn't even sound particularly surprised. "I always did wonder if you might be a little bit nuts."

CHAPTER 21

"Marion, how dare you? You're the one who's crazy! You're all crazy, all of you. I'm telling you that man tried to kill me!"

"And we are not believing you, Mrs. Druffitt," said Rhys. "You see, you have not been very clever. You have only been lucky, because you took risks somebody who was thinking straight would not have taken. I hope you will start trying to think straight now."

"I haven't the faintest idea what you're talking about," she replied with her usual hauteur.

"Then I must explain carefully, must I not? Sergeant Twofeathers, would you mind standing here next to Mrs. Druffitt? Marshal, would you be good enough to get Ben Potts on the telephone for me?"

"Sure thing." Olson, looking stunned, went to put the call through. The others clustered together, waiting. Mrs. Druffitt looked from one to the other, then averted her eyes from them all. "Ben's on the line, Inspector," he called out a moment later. "What shall I tell him?"

"I'll talk to him myself. You come back here and be prepared to assist Sergeant Twofeathers if necessary."

Rhys left the door into the hallway open behind him. Those who were waiting could hear him giving curious but explicit instructions to the undertaker. Then there was silence, a seemingly endless silence. At last Rhys spoke again.

"And you can't get it off with anything, not even steel wool? Thank you. No, that's all I wanted to know. Leave things exactly as they are. I'll be down soon."

He hung up and came back to the puzzled group. "You

see, Mrs. Druffitt, that was one of the ways in which you were not very clever. When you gave that outfit of yours to Dorothy Fewter yesterday, you should not have included the shoes."

She looked coldly down her nose at the Mountie. "Don't be ridiculous. What harm was there in giving away a pair of shoes?"

"Well, you see, that was the pair you were wearing when you came up here and left those two jars of botulinous string beans in your aunt's cellar."

"You're out of your mind! I'll have you put off the Force for this. Anybody in town can tell you that I hadn't set foot in this house for more than fifteen years, not until this very morning."

"Then anybody in town would have to be mistaken, Mrs. Druffitt, because those shoes of yours have your Uncle Charles's patent-floor cement all over the soles of them."

"That's a lie! It's white shoe polish. I spilled it while I was cleaning the shoes to give to Dot."

"You did put a great deal of polish on the shoes, but you see the polish came off when Mr. Potts wet it and the spots on the soles did not."

"Then Dot must have worn the shoes down cellar last night herself."

"Dot was not in this cellar last night. She was with Janet Wadman all evening, and later with Sam Neddick until just before she was killed. Anyway, she could not have worn them to walk so far because the shoes were too small for her. She did not have them on when she came over here from the Wadmans'. She carried them in her hand, and she did not put them on after she left Sam Neddick, either. You know what a hard time you had cramming them on her feet after you killed her, don't you? You couldn't even get the left one all the way on, because her left foot was a little bit bigger than the right, as many people's are. Yet Dot had to be wearing shoes when she was found, because it was not reasonable that anybody would mistake a barefoot woman for you, even in the dark. You would never go barefoot outdoors, would you, Mrs. Druffitt?"

"Damn right she wouldn't," Marion snorted. "Elizabeth's too respectable. She's got to uphold the family name, which is no easy job when you consider how her noble ancestors made their money, and how her uncle liked the girls and her father liked the boys and her dear old Aunt Aggie got hitched to a screwy inventor and she herself married an incompetent doctor who'd lost all his patients and was gambling away the money she needed to put on the dog with in front of a few old hens who know more about your private affairs than you do and laugh at you behind your back, like as not. Right, Elizabeth?"

Mrs. Druffitt ignored her. "I'm afraid I have to confess, Inspector, that those shoes I gave Dot were an old pair I'd had in the house for years and years. I must have got that stuff on the soles back when I still used to come here and visit Aunt Agatha."

"No you didn't, Mama," said Gilly stonily. "You bought them new a year ago last Easter. You'd never in a million years buy another pair of shoes until the old ones were past fixing."

"Gillian, how can you?"

Gilly plunged on, her voice shaking. "You had two of Aunt Aggie's jars, right down there in your own pantry. That's what you and she fought about, the time you quit speaking. I've heard the story often enough, God knows, and so had Daddy. Aunt Aggie had given you two jars of mustard pickles she'd made, and told you to be sure to give her back the jars when the pickles were gone. But you're such a miser you couldn't bring yourself to part with them, and that's how the battle started and you wound up saying you'd never set foot in the place again so you'd have an excuse not to bring them back."

"That's ridiculous!"

"I know it's ridiculous, but it's the truth all the same. I remember once when we were doing science in school I took the jars for me and Elmer to catch pollywogs in, and you raised holy hell about taking family heirlooms out of the house. You called Elmer a common thief. You remember, too, don't you, Elmer?"

Her husband nodded. "I remember."

"That's why you had to kill Daddy, isn't it, Mama? As soon as he saw that jar of green beans Janet was bringing to show him, he'd have had to admit what he'd known ever since Aunt Aggie died, wouldn't he? He must have known where those poisoned beans she ate came from, mustn't he? All he had to do was look in the pantry and notice those two jars you'd made such a rumpus about weren't on the shelf any more. He couldn't have kept on covering up for you any longer, could he? Daddy might have been sort of a jellyfish and no great shakes as a doctor, but he wasn't a complete fool."

"Was that why he said you ought to go away that day you and him had the big fight?" said Bobby. "Huh, Grandma, was it? That day you were yelling so loud?"

"Be quiet, Bobby," shrieked Mrs. Druffitt. "You don't know what you're talking about. A lady does not raise her voice!"

"Bobby, did your grandpa say 'go away' or 'be put away'?" Marion asked. "In case you don't know it, Elizabeth, you're screeching your head off right now. Sure, that's what happened, isn't it? When Janet phoned down and said she'd found something funny in the cellar that she wanted to show the doctor, you knew it must be that extra jar of beans you'd left, probably hoping I'd get hold of it and go the same way Auntie did. You didn't dare let him see the jar, so you whammed him over the head the way you did Dot, then staged your little scene and went waltzing off to your goddamn club. Boy, when it comes to nerve, you take the cake!"

Rhys interrupted. "Bobby, would you happen to recall what day it was that you heard this argument between your grandmother and grandfather?"

"Can't we keep Bobby out of this?" Gilly started to say,

but her son was not a baby any more and his grandfather had sometimes been kind to him. He answered readily enough.

"Sure, it was the day of Aunt Aggie's funeral. Grandma made me dress up in that dumb navy-blue suit she bought me when I was about eight years old, that's a mile too small."

"Where were you when you heard them talking?"

"I told you, they weren't talking. They were yelling their heads off. That's how I could hear. See, they were in the front room and I was in the pantry where she'd put the stuff left over from the party."

"Are you saying your grandmother gave a party on the day her aunt was buried?"

"Well, I guess it wasn't exactly a party. She asked people back to the house for cake and stuff after the funeral."

"Did she know you were in the pantry?"

"No, I guess not," he admitted. "Mama went home with a headache when the rest of the people left and I was supposed to go with her, but there was all this cake and stuff left so I went back again."

"You shouldn't have done that, Bobby," his mother reproved. "But he's right about the spread Mama put on, Madoc. I suppose she figured she had cause to celebrate."

"Gillian!" cried her mother. "How can you be a party to this—this dreadful slander?"

"Oh knock it off, Mama. I knew what you'd done the minute I found out the Mounties were in town. And I know why you did it. It was on account of me, wasn't it? You don't even know I exist as a human being, but you can't let go of me because you think I'm something that belongs to you. And because I'm one of your possessions, I'm supposed to be kept dusted and polished and stuck up on the mantelpiece with the rest of the knickknacks. You couldn't stand to see the way I was living because it didn't fit in with your notion of what was right and proper. When you finally had to face the fact that I wasn't going back to that torture chamber you call home, sweet home, you started conniving about getting me into the Mansion. You knew I'd inherit a share of it, but

Aunt Aggie wasn't dying fast enough to suit you so you decided to help her along."

"Gillian, you're raving! Can't you all see she must be mad?"

"Oh no, I'm not. You didn't care how many you had to kill, did you, Mama, just so you could stick me up here in this frowsy old bats' nest and be able to twitter to the ladies over the teacups about how your daughter was living in grand style up at the Mansion. When killing Daddy and Aunt Aggie didn't do the trick, you burned my own house down so I'd have no place else to go."

"Nonsense, Gillian. I was at home in my own bed when that—that hovel caught fire."

"Sure you were. But you'd lit one of those sticks of incense Bobby gave me for my birthday while I was getting dressed in the bedroom and you were out in the front room yelling at me to hurry up. You left it someplace where it would be sure to catch onto something when it burned down far enough. Then you hustled me out fast, leaving your own grandson asleep in the house. The only reason Bobby got out alive was that the fire took longer to get going than you thought it would."

"Why do you say it was incense, Gilly?" Rhys asked quietly.

"Because I can remember smelling it when I got home from Ben Potts's. I didn't think too much of it then because I was used to it. Bobby'd given me some for my birthday, you see, and we'd been burning a stick every evening because I—I wanted him to know how much I liked his present. But we had this little incense burner we always put it in, so it would have been safe enough there. Where did you put it, Mama? In that basket down behind the couch where I kept the newspapers and magazines?"

Mrs. Druffitt's lips tightened. It was clear Gilly had scored a hit. She was crying now, in shuddering gasps. "I suppose you thought it didn't matter if Bobby burned to death because he was only a B-bascom."

"If your father had had an ounce of backbone—"

"He'd have put you straight into a mental hospital where he knew damned well you belong," the daughter interrupted, "and he'd still be alive today. So would Dot Fewter. Why did you have to kill poor Dot?"

"I did no such thing! My car never left the carriage house all night. You can ask the neighbors. They'd have heard me going in and out."

"Sure they would," said Marion. "That's why you walked instead, two miles up and two miles back in the dark. That's why you were so bushed when you got here that you slept most of the day. You're not used to walking like us poor relations."

Mrs. Druffitt sniffed. "You'd say anything to get me in wrong and cover up for yourself, wouldn't you?"

"Shove it, Elizabeth! They've found your fingerprints on the rock you bashed her with."

"That's a lie! I—" the mouth snapped shut, just too late.

"I know," said Marion. "You wore gloves. Black ones, and that black dress and black shoes and black stockings like you've got on now, and a black mourning veil down over your face so that Dot wouldn't be apt to see you in the dark when she came out of the barn as you knew she would, because you're as big a gossip as she was, in your own nasty-nice way. I should have known it was you the minute I saw how carefully that rock had been put back where you got it from. Who else would be so goddamn picky?"

Marion turned to Rhys. "You go search her house. You'll find a freshly washed pair of black nylon gloves hung up to dry in the bathroom on cute little glove stretchers and you'll find an old-fashioned black net mourning veil with a heavy black border folded up in her top left-hand drawer. She'll have shaken it out, but you'll still be able to get enough dust and stuff off it to analyze, won't you, Madoc?"

"I should expect so," he replied. It was as well Marion herself hadn't turned out to be the murderess. She must read a lot of detective fiction.

Marion's voice shrilled on. "That was pretty smart, giving Dot your clothes. You knew her well enough to realize she wouldn't be able to resist wearing the dress when she came out to the barn for a roll in the hay with Sam. You just hung around in the shadows till she came out, let her have it, and left her lying there so you could start the story of somebody's trying to murder you and cover up for killing Henry and Aunt Aggie. It would have made more sense to kill me, instead, but I suppose you picked Dot because she was dumb and easy."

"Women who consort with low characters," Mrs. Druffitt began, glaring at Elmer.

"Oh shut up!" shrieked Gilly Bain. "Madoc, do you know why I've been saying these awful things against my own mother? It's because I knew when Elmer woke me up and said we were leaving that she'd done something else. I didn't ask him what it was because I couldn't bear to know. I just took my kid and went, because Elmer's the only—" she choked up, twining her tiny birdclaws over her husband's enormous hand.

"We found a nice old JP somewhere—I don't even know where—and did it right, with flowers and everything." She glanced down reverently at her battered corsage. "But when he got to the place about till death you do part, I just turned cold all over. I knew that if I let her, she'd get Elmer the way she got Daddy and Aunt Aggie."

Gilly wheeled and screamed straight in her mother's face. "Well, I'm not letting you! All my life you've been telling me what's best for me. Now I'm telling you. What's best for me is having what I've got right this minute: my kid and my dogs and a decent man to take care of us. We're going to live on what Elmer makes. I'll never touch one cent of Aunt Aggie's money. I'm signing over my share to Marion, and you've killed three people for nothing!"

Elizabeth Druffitt turned fish-belly white. Then she spoke, softly and sadly in her best Tuesday Club voice.

"How sharper than a serpent's tooth is the tongue of a thankless child."

CHAPTER 22

The bush pilot steadied the bucking single-engine plane with one hand on the controls, and reached into his pocket with the other. "Sorry, Inspector, I forgot to give you your letters."

Rhys took his eyes off the dun-colored muskeg five hundred feet below and scanned the envelopes. Two were official business, red tape winding itself clear into the middle of nowhere. The third was light blue with a deeper blue trimming on the flap, and was gracefully addressed in blue ink. That one he opened.

"Dear 'Cousin Madoc,'" Janet wrote. "It was such a pleasant surprise to get your lovely box of chocolates with the Mountie on the lid. No, of course I don't wish all Mounties looked like that one! Don't you know beauty's in the eye of the beholder?"

So it was, and a good thing, too. The muskeg began to appear a shade less drab.

"You wanted me to keep you posted on the news from Pitcherville, so here goes. My sister-in-law Annabelle and the boys are back home, and needless to say happy to be here. The kids are dreadfully upset at missing the chance to meet a real live Mountie."

It was not right to disappoint children. They might develop a trauma or something. Decidedly he had a duty to remedy that situation.

"I've decided to go back to that same job I had in Saint John. They've asked me to and at first I thought I wouldn't because of what I suppose you might call personality conflicts, but that just doesn't seem important to me any more."

The muskeg was assuming a definitely rosy hue.

"I borrowed Bert's car Friday and drove Marion up to visit Gilly and Elmer. They couldn't be happier and asked particularly to be remembered to you. It did seem a shame for Elmer to give up his place at the lumber mill, but now I realize how smart they were to get clear away from here. Elmer is doing well at his new job and they have a cute little place. Only four rooms and a sort of cubbyhole, plus a nice bathroom, but Gilly keeps it neat as the proverbial (did I spell that right?) pin, even though they have to heat with wood and you know what that means."

A teakettle at the simmer and your feet getting warm in the oven. Rhys pulled the collar of his parka up around his ears and turned the page.

"You can imagine how the tongues are wagging! Some of the ladies from the Tuesday Club went down to the hospital to visit Mrs. Druffitt and they say she's gone completely around the bend now. She told them Gilly's married to Prince Charles and they're living up at the Mansion and driving a Rolls-Royce car. She talks freely about killing Mrs. Treadway and the others . . . can't seem to recall why she did it, but is sure it was the *right thing to do!!!*

"Of course her old buddies are telling all sorts of stories now about how they always suspected Elizabeth had a screw loose somewhere because she was so determined to make everybody think the Emerys were so special when they were anything but!! Funny that nobody happened to remember that all those years when they were letting her queen it over them, wouldn't you say? I suppose the real craziness began when she got to believing it herself.

"I know I should feel charitable and forgiving toward her, but I still get boiling mad every time I think of dear old Mrs. Treadway—I do wish you could have known her!—and poor Dot Fewter getting herself dolled up to go out and get slaughtered. Oddly enough, Mrs. Fewter is taking Mrs. Druffitt's part. She thinks it's mean of Gilly not to visit her mother. She says Dot would have gone if *she'd* been the one to get put away. THAT I can believe!

"If you ask me, Gilly won't go because she's afraid her mother will have a lucid moment and say something against Elmer. She told me herself she wouldn't be able to stand that, even though she now realizes that Mrs. Druffitt was probably never 100 per cent sane. She says it still gives her the willies every time Bobby puts a stick on the fire (he's gained at least ten pounds, by the way, and looks great). She's more bothered about the murders her mother didn't commit than the ones she did. I must say I think about that sometimes, myself. Goodness knows what she might have done if you hadn't come in and stopped her! I don't know how I'll ever be able to thank you for coming to the rescue!"

Rhys had a few suggestions all lined up to make about that as soon as a suitable opportunity presented itself.

"Anyway, Pitcherville has a new *grande dame* now. The Lady of the Mansion sends her very warmest greetings. She was pretty shattered when she found out you really are a bachelor and connected with that Rhys-Brown family that used to own all those copper mines (meow!). Not that she lacks company, I must say, with Sam Neddick still camping in her hayloft and *hoping for the best!!!* And Jason Bain came chugging up the other day with a big bunch of slightly wilted flowers out of a greenhouse he'd just foreclosed on. He evidently figures if he can't get hold of the property one way, he might as well try another.

"After the peaceful summer I've had here, I'm rather looking forward to Saint John as a restful change. The girls I was living with before have taken on a new roommate so I'll be staying with a cousin of Annabelle's till I can find a place of my own. Here's her address in case you happen to be down that way and feel the urge to look me up. Having already lost my appendix, I promise I'll try not to embarrass you in public!"

As Rhys refolded the letter and tucked it carefully into his breast pocket along with other vital documents, the tiny plane hit an air pocket and dropped about two hundred feet. That was how it went in the Royal Canadian Mounted Police. You left your heart in one place and your stomach in another. He smiled tenderly down at the rose-covered muskeg and began to hum, "Oh Rose Marie, I love you."

"That's kind of a pretty tune," the pilot observed. "What is it, one of those old Welsh folk songs?"

Rhys quit humming and kept his eyes on the ground. They'd be landing soon. Somewhere down on that apparently barren wasteland, the quarry he'd followed so far from Fredericton was waiting. He didn't intend to lose much more time on this case. As soon as he'd got his man and reported back to headquarters, he had a really tough assignment to tackle. Somehow, he must wangle a pass down to Saint John and get his woman.